Penguin Books
## PAPER NAUTILUS

NICHOLAS JOSE was born in 1952 and grew up in South Australia. He has since lived and worked in various parts of Australia (mainly Canberra) and in England, Italy and China. His books include two collections of short stories, *The Possession of Amber* and *Feathers or Lead*, and a novel, *Rowena's Field*.

Also by the author

*The Possession of Amber* (1980)
*Rowena's Field* (1984)
*Feathers or Lead* (1986)

# PAPER NAUTILUS

Nicholas Jose

PENGUIN BOOKS

assisted by the Literature Board of the Australia Council

Penguin Books Australia Ltd,
487 Maroondah Highway, P.O. Box 257
Ringwood, Victoria 3134, Australia
Penguin Books Ltd,
Harmondsworth, Middlesex, England
Penguin Books,
40 West 23rd Street, New York, N.Y. 10010, U.S.A.
Penguin Books (Canada) Limited,
2801 John Street, Markham, Ontario, Canada L3R 1B4
Penguin Books (N.Z.) Ltd,
182-190 Wairau Road, Auckland 10, New Zealand

First published by Penguin Books Australia, 1987

Copyright © Nicholas Jose, 1987

All Rights Reserved. Without limiting the rights under copyright reserved above, no part of this publication may be reproduced, stored in or introduced into a retrieval system, or transmitted, in any form or by any means (electronic, mechanical, photocopying recording or otherwise), without the prior written permission of both the copyright owner and the above publisher of this book.

Typeset in 11/12 Garamond by Midland Typesetters, Maryborough 3465
Made and printed in Australia by The Book Printer, Maryborough, Victoria

**CIP**

Jose, Nicholas, 1952- .
Paper nautilus.
ISBN 0 14 010019 9.
I. Title.
A823'.3

Creative writing program assisted by the Literature Board of the Australia Council, the Federal Government's arts funding and advisory body.

In memory of my mother, Pamela Violet Jose.

# CONTENTS

1 • A WEDDING, FEBRUARY 1965     1
2 • THE BOY, SUMMER 1961     11
3 • DRIFT, 1953     29
4 • THE ROAD, 1946-1950     59
5 • BISCUIT, JUNE-JULY 1945     87
6 • SPINNER, 1941-1945     119

'Even if only one good memory is left in our hearts, it may also be the instrument of our salvation one day.'

Alyosha Karamazov

# 1 • A WEDDING, FEBRUARY 1965

WHEN HE THOUGHT OF PEACE HE thought of a particular tree on a promontory across the bay – a ball on a stick, such as a child might draw. Sometimes so close that he could almost grasp it in the palm of his hand, at other times a blur on the horizon, the tree was the point inside himself where all things came together.

The wedding was a happy one. The roses were out and people danced with gusto in the warm air, their hearts full. When the speeches were over the guests drank and spun until one girl with no underpants on upturned the trestle table, and herself, showing that not everyone was taking Rob and Penny's sanctified road.

Jack Tregenza also took another road that night. As soon as the bride and groom had left, he drove to the old shack and his comfy banana chair on the porch, to wait for dawn and his tree: and now, in the morning, the beach and day were quiet, the water lapped in a gentle alternation of withholding and surrender, and he squinted into the light as his feelings moved between emptiness and satisfaction.

'I've waited years to hear Penny say "I do",' Rob had said forthrightly in his speech, clamping his hands to the tabletop. 'We better make sure it's been worth waiting for.' His mates hooted and Penny's smile suggested obstacles overcome. Perhaps they had not waited, in the literal sense. Jack never again saw such passion as between them at the beginning – but Penny had been a stern teenager, prepared to wait for the real things to come. Now her presence helped Rob not to falter as he thanked the bridesmaids, 'for being almost as beautiful as the bride', the lewd best man 'for his helpful hints', the minister, his mum and dad, and Mr Tregenza, 'to whom my special thanks are due, for throwing such a terrific do, and for taking care of Penny. You saw her through.' The wedding crowd clapped, beholding Penny strong and healthy in front of them, her own woman, ready to share her capacities with the boy. For Jack, that tribute was poetry enough. He was no wordsmith. He couldn't get his foot out of his mouth to broadcast feelings he had never named anyway. So Les Hocking, who had known Penny all her life, stood up to do the speechifying, and had them all in stitches.

Glamorous Vera, on Stan Petchek's arm, was done up to outshine the bride. Taking advantage of the evening's goodwill, she had several times over told the story of her life to the curious, insincere people of Wooka. Out of earshot someone said, 'Jack's all the *real* family Penny's got.'

During the last hymn, as he walked down the aisle in the newlywed's train, Jack had felt bereft in the midst of everyone's delight. Penny was walking away from him, hurrying out of the church in a rustle of white, away from girlhood and all the past, and if he lifted a finger to stop her, or did other than grin, the lean young man on her arm would battle him. Rob Stewart had taken his helpmeet, and the conviction of Penny's 'I do' shocked the congregation. She had waited until she could mean it, when her girlish desire had turned towards the surety of 'honour and obey', as Rob honoured her in all his life's plans. Only, the words rent Jack Tregenza because she was going.

In a gesture of the hand he had passed the girl across and stepped back from the altar. Her hair was thick and yellow, her skin slightly tanned. She was frank and plump in the girdling white dress, more matter-of-fact than ceremonious. Jack was pleased as punch to present her in church. Kneeling, he gave scant thought to the couple's future. That was another story. Instead his thoughts moved back through the twenty years' past that flowed into this present. Standing, he sang out: *Goodness and mercy all my days/ Will surely follow me* . . ., and blood came to the surface of his skin. The little organ played. In the packed country church farmers in stretched best suits and ladies in flowers and sheen and sparkle shuffled and hemmed, singing an ancient hymn of death and harvest.

The house bustled on the wedding morning with girls closeted to wash, braid and pin while older women under Kath Hocking's command laid the tables, carted baskets and did flowers. Outside, Les Hocking was helping Jack to wire the lights.

'It's all turned out pretty well,' said Les. 'What do you see yourself doing now?'

Jack estimated. 'Nothing different to what I'm doing already.'

'You're still a young fella, don't forget. Whoops!' Les's ladder rocked under him.

Jack didn't feel young, though. Epochs had passed imperceptibly in his squat house of dusty stone, neither grey nor yellow, speckled with mica. He knew every tree and shrub of the place, each gate, each tap, each bit of guttering, each rusty implement that had never been fixed or sold. Since his mother died he had lived there sixteen years as sole master, both father and mother to young Penny. The house had been his mother's girlhood home too, but the family had never gathered there in the usual sense, in one time and place. Their wholeness was spread tenuously across the years. As he went about the garden Jack was stirred by memories of those whom the shrubs had outlived. Prodigiously watered for the February wedding, the lawn was a commemorative, heraldic green.

He went and got the Saint Christopher from the desk drawer, and took it to the room where the girls were giggling.

'Pen?'

She shook her head so her hair fell in a mess over her eyes. 'It's hopeless! Bloody hair! We'll have to start again, kids.' She pulled her robe round and strode into the hall.

'Penny, here's the Saint Christopher for your something old,' Jack said. 'Careful not to lose it.'

The gold medallion was smaller than her little fingernail, flat and worn, with tooth marks in it. The miniature Saint Christopher, his colossal legs planted in the stream, his barrel chest bearing forward, had on his shoulders the baby Christ whose hands were open in a shadowing of the cross.

'It's yours to keep. For good luck. If its luck hasn't run out already. Hang on to it and let's hope things go your way.'

He had overreached himself and she kissed him. 'I'm a bundle of nerves.' She looked placid enough, ruddy and freckled. 'I keep thinking it's now or never if I want to go back on it. I *don't* want to, but what if something came over me? I've thought and thought.'

She was standing in the sun. She held her destiny in her hand as if it were a pebble she could evaluate, turn, drop, clench in her fist. She was rocking on her heels, to and fro, before the wedding claimed her.

'I'll be very proud of you, darling,' said Jack with a squeeze.

She had presented Jack with a scroll and a photo of herself in a starched white nurse's uniform, having achieved the goal for which she went up to town; she hated waste. If her abilities had once suggested something greater, she now believed there was nothing finer than the work of easing distress. Creditable exam results secured her a job in the local hospital, and she had come home, as always, to the house, the farm, the southern peninsula, and Uncle Jack, who kept her safe as long as she remembered. In her own right now, with her own qualification, she would sow and reap what was in store. Keen and bright, like a sprouting seed, she turned her face to the sun as they sat on the beach. She wore zinc cream on her nose, sunglasses and a ponytail, and turned her eyes out to sea, away from Uncle Jack, and from Rob who sprawled beside her. He was another reason why she had returned.

Penny sat squarely on the towel with her knees up. Rob lay on his back with his body inclined towards her so he could stroke her smooth, oiled calf unobserved. In time she took his hand and he was content, not thinking but frowning, not looking but dreaming. He knew the difficulties ahead would make him strong, and when he and Penny were old, whatever weights hung from their bootlaces, their story would be a measure of toughness. She had already taught him so much, and his promises were unshakably firm. His fingers rubbed her thigh and she relaxed towards him, then twisted round to speak over her shoulder, 'Uncle Jack, Rob and I have something to tell you.'

The conventional form brought his focus from the distant azure dance to the young couple blushing beside him on the sand.

'Yep,' said Rob, whose place it was to speak, 'we want to get married.' His dark eyes twinkled as he flushed deeper at the words. 'At long last.'

'About time indeed,' said Jack who got to his feet and brushed himself down to offer a hand to young Rob. 'Congratulations, boy. I'm glad you're going ahead with it. It's great news, darling,' he gushed as he gave Penny a hug. He was clumsy, embarrassed, and his eyes screwed up.

'Well,' he said, uncovering his face and rubbing his hands. 'There's a lot to talk about. A great deal.' He clapped his hands above his head and the stalking seagulls took to the air. 'You kids have finally done it,' said Jack Tregenza. He felt weightless himself, soaring on wings above the mirror surface of the planet.

Then he settled on his towel and purposefully tucked his legs under. Penny and Rob did likewise.

Poor old Uncle Jack. He was sturdy and trim, with stocky, shock-absorbent legs. No one in Wooka thought of *him* as young, or agile, or marriageable. They were used to his navy-blue cardigan behind the desk at the stock and station agency, and his quiet sorting of brochures when a farmer came in with a query, and the way his hands pressed the air when there was a difficulty about payment, as if all difficulties were air, and how in extremes he pressed the seasoned desk-top to take the resistance on himself. He was an honest mediator between the stubborn farmers and the companies' push into ever-new chemicals and machines. If he was sometimes wrong, no one could be right all the time in a world where lies were honoured in glossy print. Jack was in the habit of advising caution, with the wisdom that on the land nothing ever changed really. In the community he had an old man's responsibility that he bore cheerfully, but you couldn't get him to let his hair down with the larrikin element in the pub. His well-groomed hair was already silvered.

The farm which Jack ended up with had not been intended for him, and he didn't take it seriously. He pottered about there as a hobby, relying on day labour in busy times. In Jack's mother's day the good soil of the farm had supplied all of Wooka with milk, and Irene Tregenza, née Platt, had worked herself into the grave as a cow lady, even after she married a fisherman, even after her son got started on a desk job. Generations of prime manure enriched the soil of Platts' farm. Even in the worst seasons, years after the cows had gone, there was still good feed.

But although he would have been an excellent catch, the women of Wooka had stopped considering Jack as a prospect. Thus a bachelor becomes confirmed and part of the established order. Uncertainty and distrust fade. He becomes mate to men, flirt to women, uncle to children, and a decent bloke instead of a coot.

The 'boys' shack' was how he still referred to his place on the beach, one fibro room that the weather had worn to the dusty grey of the surrounding saltbush and the stones, where the cliff dropped to sand and water of a variant green. Inside, it was partitioned into an eating area and two small sleeping spaces. The floor was concrete. It was a beloved place, tranquilly preserved. For drinking water there was a crusty tank on a tower over the laundry shed, and that was enough. Under a rough bed was the set of deck quoits the boys had thrown in youth, when moon-faced Jack had never been happier.

Jack was peculiar in the district because he had brought up young Penny by himself, as if she was his own. No one expected it of him. He could easily have refused. But that was how it came about and now he had a girl to give away in marriage.

'Pen and I can manage, Mr Tregenza. I reckon there's no obstacle.' Since his twenty-first birthday, Rob's utterances had become more meagre and more solemn. 'I'm getting a decent wage from the old man. I've got the block. There's the other house there, not fantastic, till we can build something of our own on it. There's all them trees – the windbreak. We won't be under mum and dad's nose. If Pen can get herself a job at the hospital there's no problems until our circumstances change.'

Rob's family had a place on the road out from Wooka. Old Man Stewart was frugal, with a clannish code of honour that looked after his own kind. His rumoured wealth would come, in the grinding of time, to Rob and Rob's brother, if neither blotted the escutcheon. Meanwhile they would be made to serve. These tough conditions had made Rob optimistic and self-appraising. He knew his capacity and broached his engagement to Penny

Tregenza as a grand yet realistic scheme. Jack only worried that Penny would be pressed too close to the Stewarts' bosom, but that was no bad thing for a girl whose own family had been dislocated. A single child, Penny had often depended on the graces of strangers. She knew how to resist when necessary. Besides, Uncle Jack was always there, a fount of love, if she needed him.

So it was settled, and only the lighter matters remained to muse over: the day of the wedding, the time, the place, the dress, the doings, who would come – and whether Vera would be invited. The sun was low over the water as they talked, and their eyes tired from the level glare.

'I could go a beer,' said Rob Stewart, pulling Penny to her feet. She stood apart from him to enjoy the sense of accomplishment, as firm as the sand beneath her feet. She had taken a single step into maturity, following the curve of her life. She remembered the feeling from former times, as she wiggled her toes down into the wet sand and smiled at both men.

'Come on.'

As they climbed down to the beach that afternoon, Jack had guessed there was an accord between the young ones. No clues were given as they grilled their chops and sausages and laughed about the holidays. Penny had to goad Rob into speaking.

To give them time, Jack went for a long, solitary, delicious swim. Discreetly he watched the lovers on the shore. They would raise a family of their own while he would swim on as he did today, breast-stroking placidly with bursts of freestyle, once Penny was set free and his only ties were to the sea and sky and land. He remembered playing with his brother on the same sand beneath the shack. It hadn't changed much. The old gnarled she-oak was older and more gnarled. A great undulating branch now covered the roof and tucked its fingers under the guttering in a complete embrace. The roots reached down into the cliff and seemed to carry the crust of land beneath the shack, which from seaward looked like a cubby-house in the branches of one giant tree.

Reminded of his own extension, Jack kicked his distant feet as if they were fins. He thought of the sandpipers that ran in crazy fast lines across the sand left by receding waves. When the sandpipers stopped, it was never to consider, only to redirect themselves and scamper on. Now Jack had all the time in the world for considering, for trying to grasp how far and long the line was from his first memory. He rolled away from the shore and looked to his particular tree across the bay. The tree had always been there, a beacon. Jack imagined: If he had been the fisherman who stood under that tree long ago, casting a line into the future, and if now, swimming in the sea, he was the fish that took the lure, then as the reel was wound in he would be pulled through the water towards that distant point, drawn back through a whole lifetime.

## 2 • THE BOY, SUMMER 1961

AT FIFTEEN PENNY TREGENZA WAS sent away to school. She didn't argue at the rupture. As a changeling child she never presumed to challenge her circumstances, accommodating herself to a world that proved to be home: Uncle Jack, the southern peninsula, the squat square house and the fat paddocks, the land's end and the little grey shack overlooking the bay; the faces old and young watching her sidelong, remembering, all her days; the weatherboard school where she was content to do well (without exertion), the girls who discussed boys incessantly, boys who never lifted a finger for the girls.

Because he had a wider view, Jack sent his girl to a ladies' boarding school in Adelaide where she would study for her Leaving certificate. As the major influence on her life, he was aware of his own inadequacies. There were things only women could teach. Jack had overcompensated with love, and never knew that Penny profited richer than rubies.

He chose the ladies' college as a cloister from the worst of what the city offered. He was wrong. The school's unexpressed purpose was to initiate girls to the dainty, perfumed rough-and-tumble of a lady's life. Snobbery, money, keeping up, grooming and deportment, the fear of plainness or oddness, sighting a prospect, chasing, clawing: such were the lessons learned.

Penny was not taken in. However, she could not read about life without becoming aware of danger as part of its stake. She discovered heroes and heroines – Cleopatra, Jeanne d'Arc, Napoleon, E. B. Browning – to be emulated in a girl's afterlife, in Adelaide, on a property, on the boulevards of Paris or in the squares of London, for these were now places on her map.

The broadest horizon was still the bay. She got a prize for improvement at the speech day and afterwards Jack drove her home. The black road shimmered in the December heat, low eucalypts pressed towards her and golden paddocks of full-headed grain swam in her eyes. Soon she smelled the salt and saw the sandhills between road and shore. The track rose straight between long fences over a high sown hill, and at the top was the sweep of the bay with its contours of virgin blue and darker blue, a running fringe of white, and trawlers at rest in the jetty's lee. After being away she had points of comparison, words and images for a gentle shore that was paradise before paradise was ever heard of. Any visitor who did not feel the same had not grown up there from first breath, was not returning from an epic year in the crowded places of the world. Penny was half sophisticated now, bursting with the warm pulsation of air and cloud, paddock and mottled wave.

Jack had been lonely while she was away. He did not recognize the sluggish unhappiness that coiled around him that year. A kind of pining, unaware of its object, made him snap uncustomarily, like a dull drizzle that sets in for winter. At night he would use any groaning roof or whistling fence as an excuse for getting up and walking about in his pyjamas to frighten off the prowlers from his mind. To writhing in bed he preferred the quietened night world of stars or cloud; in the daytime he looked haggard to those who could see. That was when Jack Tregenza started to be old, wrestling at night with the angel of emptiness in his arms.

For Penny's return he repainted the woodwork in her room and put his best African violet by her bed. When she threw open her case, he wondered if he would have to make extra shelving for the books, magazines, clothes and cosmetics that came tumbling out. There was an atomizer that she tested in the air for his benefit. There were pictures to tape on the wall.

'That's pretty jazzy,' he said, when a carton revealed a hard bright plastic record-player.

'A present from Vera for doing so well.'

'Did she send it?'

'She took me out to lunch. She took me to the Bohemian Restaurant on North Terrace and bought me stockings that I hate and nail polish.' She made a comic face. 'You should've seen her.'

'No thanks.'

Her presence recovered his purpose.

After work he would put on old clothes and they would go about the garden, Penny talking. Next year, next year . . . She was definitely going back for Leaving Honours. She had been assistant stage manager for the school play and would be stage manager next year. Their hockey team was second in the tournament and her best friend would be captain next year. After next year she would go to the university to study law. There was no reason why a woman shouldn't be a barrister. She could see herself in court, like Portia. All hail to the modern world! Those who died for freedom had not died in vain if the young could inherit a world of such scope. Next year . . . . It was easier to contemplate the summer that intervened.

The sun baked the flesh and the garden responded to their touch. That Christmas the hibiscus were the finest ever: masses of little papery trumpets, flame coloured, salmon, brick and blush coloured, creamy white and bloody crimson, single and double, Jack's pride and joy. He had overcome his distaste for the slimy stench as they rotted, the whiff of bodies in decay. Now they were sweet flowers he managed to grow with difficulty in his limey garden.

At dusk, Penny and Jack would go inside and drink a beer in the kitchen while she prepared the food – steak or fish and salad, and the local fresh bread, ice cream, tinned pears and chocolate sauce – nothing fancy. She had made him get a television set for his solitary evenings. A huge aerial was erected to pick up the transmission from Adelaide. But Jack seldom settled to stare at world events through the black-and-white snow. Penny wanted to discuss politics. From her school debating, she was full of the communist threat – a new worry for Jack Tregenza. She introduced instant coffee after dinner and he allowed himself a nightcap of port. Occasionally he declared that science was the way of the future. He slept like a baby in those days, in the cocoon of knowing that Penny was in her room, playing rock-and-roll records till all hours, and would still be there in the morning.

For Christmas Eve they moved across to the shack and kept vigil on the verandah, in darkness so as not to attract insects. The night was star bright and they could see with insect eyes. Black *wok-wok* beetles soldiered over the cement towards them. Further along the beach they could see holidaymakers' bonfires. They could see lamps on the water where waders were looking for flounder, or moving faster where boats were out dabbing for garfish, and the southern stars brighter than all the lights, thicker than swarming bees.

'You know, it's so calm,' said Jack, 'you could be forgiven for believing it's been like this from time immemorial. Not so. One Christmas Eve she blew up like the worst storm you'd ever get in winter. Worse because it was so completely out of season that no one was prepared. No one could give credence. You couldn't open the front door against the wind. Six-foot-high waves in the bay coming right up against the cliff. A real freak. Peter and I were out in the boat with Dad. Nineteen thirty-four it was. I'd have been about ten, I reckon. Dad had taken the trawler round to Parawurlie Bay with us boys to get some cray for the festive season. She was flat enough when we set out, but not right, a weird milky calm like something was fuming there. We remembered afterwards. She started blowing up when we were just out of Parawurlie, but you couldn't believe it would be anything. You'd have been daft to go back. In those days even if someone had a vehicle you had a rough job getting out from Parawurlie overland. Dad reckoned it would be easier round Point Light – slow going alright – and once we got past the lighthouse the sea got worse. The big trawler was a toy, and the spray was *hot* – that was the strange thing – hot water coming down drenching us from over our heads. Still, the boat kept going thank the Lord, and Peter and I hung on for dear life. I remember grabbing his ankle one time so he wouldn't be swept off, and another time he grabbed on to mine. Dad yelled out that us boys had to fend for ourselves because he needed all his wits to bring the boat in. We were truly rocking and rolling then.

'We just kept going somehow. The old man had a sixth sense when it came to direction. Somehow he pointed her right. Suddenly Peesey Point was there to starboard and we were crashing towards the jetty. That was a close shave. The whole place was out shouting and carrying on. Once we made the lee we threw out the anchor and jumped into the dinghy to scramble on shore. We were washed sideways, but what did it matter? Your Granny Irene was there with the old Vauxhall. She'd spent half the day and all the night worried sick. At three-thirty in the morning, Dad came wading out of the sea carrying the sack of crays he promised to get. Irene scolded him before she said a word of welcome. She grabbed Peter and me by the scruff of our ratty necks, whisked us to the car, pulled off our sodden clothes and wrapped blankets round us. Then she slipped Dad a hipflask of scotch. She was crying, I remember, as wet as the weather. She had given us up for dead, all three. "The best

Christmas present I've ever had, Willie Tregenza," she said, biting her lip, "and never again!" '

'I can remember Irene biting her lip,' said Penny, 'not letting you see that something was wrong, then smiling wonderfully.'

'It's funny,' said Jack. 'Peter and I were sitting in the car while Dad conferred with the grown-ups on the beach about what to do with the boat, because it wasn't properly moored, and in that short space of time the light came up. The wind dropped just like that. The sea died down. It happened instantly, as if ordered to stop. By six o'clock the sun was shining, the sky was blue, the sea was back to its usual mild chop, only all churned up. The beach was a mess, trees uprooted, weed, bushes, shags, cuttlefish, all strewn together. But already it was like a hot summer's day. No one would believe it who wasn't there. The Wooka pub opened at seven o'clock that Christmas morning. The whole mob arrived for a few grogs before church. Peter and me got a bottle of stout to drink 'cause we were the heroes. We had mountains of beautiful crayfish to eat that day.'

Their own Christmas was different. Jack slept heavily in the little back room away from the sea. Penny woke early in the front bed when the sun flooded in making the bed too hot. In bare feet and cotton nightie she crept across the floor and put the kettle on. Waiting for the water to boil, she stared through the screen door at the opal sleepy sea and hugged herself. The movement of the globe, and of history, made this dawn particular.

She took two mugs of tea to Jack's shadowy room and shook his shoulder where he lay on his side on the iron-frame bed, breathing deeply. His body gave off heat.

'Happy Christmas, Uncle Jack,' she said eagerly.

He twisted round to face her through his sleep, rubbing his screwed-up eyes. 'Happy Christmas,' he smiled, putting his big arm round her neck to pull her down for a kiss.

'Wait,' she said. Quickly she fetched her present and

settled comfortably against him while he opened it. She nestled into his chest as she had done as a child. He folded back the paper and shook out what was inside, a thick brown jumper that she had been knitting for months.

'Try it on.'

'It's too hot!'

'Go on,' she said excitedly. 'I'm terrified it won't fit. I copied one of your old ones, but I think you've got fatter.'

He sat up and pulled the jumper over his head. Then he rolled out of bed, tightened his pyjama cord, and modelled for her.

'Fits perfectly, eh? You're very clever, darling.'

'I am clever,' she said smugly, drinking her tea.

'Well if you're so clever, miss, see if you can find what I've got for *you*.' He propped himself against the wall with his arms crossed. 'It's somewhere in this room.'

Penny pulled a long face. 'That's not *giving*.'

There was next to nothing in the room. Under the bedframe with its thin mattress was nothing but an empty suitcase. A small chest; a single wardrobe like a broom cupboard, piled full of old magazines, with a mirror on the door. Over the window was a sun-bleached yellow curtain printed with faded red-and-blue yachts that had been there since Jack was a boy. On the wall was a chart of deep-sea fish in descending sizes. Nowhere to hide a present.

'Steady on,' cried Jack as Penny started to toss the socks and handkerchieves about in the drawer.

'Hmph! I'm not giving up.'

'You're getting warm,' he said as she picked up her mug from the bedside chair.

'It's not on your person, I hope?'

'Not exactly.'

'I'll tickle you to make you tell me. I'll torture you!' she squealed, lungeing at her uncle.

He held her by the elbows as her fists beat against his chest.

'Think hard,' he instructed with a toothy smile. 'Where was the Saint Christopher hidden? You know the story.'

Jack had a wide-brimmed straw sunhat, a coolie's hat, sitting on top of the wardrobe.

'Errh,' growled Penny. 'That's not fair because I can't see that high.'

'You need the chair.'

Climbing up, she lifted the hat and found the parcel. 'It's not very big.'

She sat with Jack on the bed as she unwrapped it.

'Now that you're a serious student,' he said, 'with a future. Do you like it?'

It was a gold fountain pen on which her initials were engraved. She buried her face against Uncle Jack's neck, suddenly went coy and pulled away. She drew her legs up and clasped her knees, and her hair covered her eyes. To be given an adult present was wonderful!

Jack stretched, and his bare toes touched hers. He hardly dared move. He had played with her all his life, and she was full of intensities he could scarcely guess at.

'Drink your tea,' he said, looking at his watch. 'Church time.'

'The weather's too nice for church,' Penny complained. 'I'd rather have a swim.' She didn't want to announce that she had started to disbelieve.

'For old times' sake,' he said. He wasn't pleading, nor would he resort to the blackmail of love. 'If we don't put in an appearance, they'll think we've gone bush.'

'Who cares?'

Church was a simple affair. The people were comfortable in themselves, as in their pews, and there was no embarrassment about the free drop of wine and the wafer. Conscience-searching in Wooka was confined to neighbours' scrutiny, with eyes practised at sizing up stock. Afterwards they stood about under the noble line of gums on the hill that marked the church. A group of young 'uns appraised Penny in silence. Decently she stayed by her uncle. 'Doesn't she look gorgeous,' said Kath Hocking to Jack, insisting that they come home for Christmas dinner. 'I've got food for an army – eh, Les?'

But Jack spread his arm across Penny's shoulder to claim her, ignoring the shadow of her reluctance. Once they were back at the shack, in the blazing heat of the still morning, with the lustrous sea and the chook spitting in the pan, cold beer on the card table on the verandah, they were glad to be the elect of light and air.

In the afternoon, figures began to appear on the beach, free for their holidays. Family groups settled under awnings. Old people strolled along the shore in pairs. Children tried out their Christmas clobber. Teenagers drove out from Wooka to release themselves off the rocks into the clear deep water.

While her uncle dozed, Penny went to swim with kids she had known since childhood. They welcomed her warily, since she had been away. To swim underwater was easier, with eyes open to observe zebra fish and clay-coloured mullet paler than their shadows on the white sea floor. She was out far when a black goggled head with a snorkel aimed at her. Suddenly the head went under. She didn't believe anyone could hold their breath so long, or travel so far, beneath the surface.

Only a little space away the exultant harpoon speared into the air with a flapping trophy of fish. The boy came after, pulled up his goggles, shook his head and swore. 'A blasted tiddler. They're much bigger underwater. S'pose I should throw it back,' he called out, mocking. She laughed. 'The big fish will eat it if it's bleeding, but. Too bad. Least give the thing a chance.'

Deftly he prised out the prongs. The fish was stunned, then wriggled drunkenly.

'It's fantastic to get one at all,' consoled Penny.

'I s'pose,' he snorted. 'Bloody things sit on the bottom like sitting ducks. It's not that hard to pick 'em off.

Some get up to three or four pounders.'

He was not used to talking to strangers, or girls, or anyone at all really. He heard himself say, 'You stopping down here?'

'Up there,' she pointed.

He nodded. His dark crew cut was a wet spiky fur of little spines. He had dark eyes, tufty eyebrows, and a long, swarthy, serious face. He was sixteen and a half.

The boy signalled a provisional farewell and swam away. Penny sidestroked to the beach, pleased with the encounter as she picked her way round rocks and rockpools to the sand in front of the shack. She acknowledged him later when he walked past. He was shy. He didn't know what to do with himself. Lanky, muscly, he was a brown stick in the distance.

That evening she sat mooning on the verandah while Jack also dreamed, sentimental given the chance.

'I'll be hitting the sack early,' he said.

'Me too.'

She gave a little yawn.

The boy was Rob Stewart. He was at the beach next morning when she came down the steps with her uncle. He called out 'G'day'. He was playing a ball game in the water with his cousins, the most loutish of whom threw the ball at Penny. Jack intercepted and tossed it back with boyish glee. But Penny swam in the opposite direction, not wanting to join in.

She was face down on her towel when Rob came up and started putting questions. What was she doing? Did she want to go for a walk?

'Will you be here this afternoon?' he asked, slouching.

'Yeah, this afternoon.'

'Hey Rob!' yelled his cousins from the water. When he rejoined them, there was a burst of laughter. When she thought about boys, Penny decided that Rob was an exception – he was chivalrous and decent.

In the subsequent days they walked and swam and went

out in the boat. One night he came round to listen to records and they sat on the bed talking and talking until Penny was worried that Uncle Jack would be kept awake and hear. But Jack did a good job of snoring audibly.

They played the same records and said the same things until at midnight, as at a signal, Rob took hold of Penny's hand, leaned across and flatly kissed her lips. Gently she pushed him away. Even the brush of his mouth was a shock. She indicated her uncle behind the partition. Rob kissed her again. Neither quite understood how their short, pure courtship had been leading to this.

'No,' mouthed Penny, 'you better go.' It was loud enough for Jack to hear.

'Yeah,' Rob mumbled, straightening himself.

'Gee the tide's out far,' he said, when they were outside. She followed him down and they sauntered across the wide cold sand to the silvery water's edge. Standing against her, Rob put his hands on her shoulders, gripped her in his hard arms and kissed her until she felt dizzy. He was delicious. He kissed her neck and ears, and squeezed her until she would break. She was in love with him, and couldn't let go of his hand when at last he pulled away.

'Tomorrow.'

Head bowed, he was vanishing in the starlight. She heard the low rumble of stones and, after an interval, his whistling. She curled her toes in the sweetest dream.

Next morning he banged on the door at ten o'clock.

'I'm afraid she's still asleep, Rob. Come in.'

The boy was not prepared for that. He had come under a compulsion. Nor was Jack Tregenza prepared for Penny's first beau, and was excessively affable. He was surprised too when Penny emerged sleepy headed to tell Rob to wait five minutes, and in less than five minutes was ready without a protest.

So quick! Jack had had no chance for love as a youth. The war had come before all that fiddle, stealing his passion. Afterwards he had not let himself. Then there were Irene's salty lectures – 'Watch out, my boy. Keep yourself to yourself' – and Peter's experience, getting caught. Jack laughed about the women who wanted to rescue him – he was always too much of a duffer to say yes. Until now he did not consider what he had been denied. Besides, there was Penny.

Penny and tongue-tied Rob were in a diving-bell of their own. To find out what they were doing, Jack had to knock on glass. She would promise to be back at a certain time, definitely in time for a meal; then she would cut it fine, or her watch would have stopped, or she would come at the end of the day to ask if Rob could stay for tea. The boy giggled as Penny reverently served his plate, touching his shoulder like a parody of a mother. And when he wasn't around, she spent hours doing herself up for him. It was life with a mooncalf – yet Jack was thankful.

Towards the end of the holiday, the stock and station agency reopened. The summer was at its most splendid, so Penny stayed on at the shack, and Jack came out at the end of each day. Though he was glad to be back at work, the problems piled on his desk made him grumpy. The first evening he came home to a scrap of paper from Penny on the kitchen table, saying she'd gone to a barbecue with Rob. He poured himself a beer and wondered whether he could be bothered to cook a meal for one. He ate a lump of bread and butter and poured another beer, opening another bottle before he made up his mind. It was ridiculous to be so miserable. All the year she had been away and he had coped. But he had grown used to her being in his life again, and now that she was absent, taken, the raging hurt of his loss made him realize his joy in her. Jack's emotion got quickly out of control. He could not think back or imagine forward to any consoling perspective. She was only fifteen. What if something happened to her? You could trust Rob up to a certain point, but these young lads didn't have much sense, not if he was showing off, not if he'd had a bit of booze. He would force himself on her like a tireless puppy. God knows what sort of mess they would get into: she was so gone on the boy. Jack poured himself another beer, worried sick, and decided the best thing was to drive to the place where Rob was staying and calmly have a word with whoever was in charge. He wouldn't embarrass her, he'd just call in casually . . .

Through the open door of the shack down the road, Jack saw Old Man Stewart and his wife playing cards with the boy's aunt and uncle. They were suspicious people of few words. Ignoring Jack's evident anxiety, they offered him a sociable chair and said that the kids had gone off in one of the cars for a barbecue tea on the beach. 'Your Penny,' said Old Man. Jack was pale and furious, keeping his composure. He said it was nothing important – to tell Penny to come on home if they saw her – and gave a brisk cheerio and left. He would have squashed any rabbit that hopped into his headlights on the way home. Little Penny, his charge, his darling, gone without counsel, God knows where.

As he lay on his bare bed in the darkness of the shack, his nightmares came to the surface of his mind, all the fears dammed up behind his responsibility for the gift of Penny. He was almost in a frenzy when in the small hours of the morning there was the languorous melody of her voice at the door saying goodnight to Rob. In her muffled tones he heard the summer magic of youthful love, their lips touching, the rustle of goodbye. In the surge of his relief, Jack forgave them everything.

'That you, Pen?' he called when she came inside.

'Yes,' she whispered. 'Sorry I'm late, Uncle Jack. Talk to you in the morning. I've got to sleep.'

All that night Jack stared at the ceiling, frightened by the depth he had uncovered in his feelings for Penny. Thank God he was given a chance to learn.

No one ever knew that through the hottest weeks of

that summer Jack Tregenza loved his niece with a fervour that he thought would consume him. He never said a word or made a sign as day after day, night after agonizing night, Penny went off with young Rob Stewart. She wasn't his to keep. Nor did he allow himself curiosity, when even the most innocent questions came out wrong –

'Where are you going tonight? What do you and Rob find to talk about all the time?'

She was sensitive enough to say, 'I promise I'll spend tomorrow night at home,' but come tomorrow she would say, 'Rob might drop around after tea. That's alright, isn't it? We'll just watch the television.' And they would sit awkwardly in the living room until Jack had the grace to go to bed.

Only once there might have been a scene, a drowsy, humming Sunday afternoon when Penny and Rob had gone off to play tennis and Jack went to the shack for a swim. When he returned towards teatime, the young ones were already back, their drained cups and tea things on the kitchen table. Wondering where they were, Jack determined not to go looking and ambled to his study instead. He found Penny and Rob bent over his desk there. The study was a room where Penny would not normally go. A drawer was open. When Jack's eyes fell on the tiny Saint Christopher medallion glinting between the boy's fingers, he went prickly all over. He blurted, before Penny had a chance to speak,

'You're not giving him the Saint Christopher!'

Penny started, and stared. It was Rob who spoke.

'She's just showing me, Mr Tregenza.'

They were nervous and uncertain, as if there were guilt. 'You were out, Uncle Jack. I was telling Rob about the Saint Christopher and wanted to show him. I'm sorry for going into your study without permission.'

Rob's face was long and angry. He touched Penny's arm. 'I better be going.'

After she saw him off, Penny slumped down opposite

Jack in the living room.

'I can't always keep it a secret,' she said. 'Sometimes I have to tell. But how could you imagine I would just give it away like that? Anyway, if I did want to give it away, I would. I would know what I was doing, Uncle Jack. I would be free to give someone the most precious thing if it was right.'

'You're only fifteen.'

'What's that got to do with it?'

'You're so thick with the boy anything could happen. I hope you know what you're doing, that's all. People get fired up and rue the consequences. Think of Vera and poor Peter.'

'My parents.'

She gulped, turned and ran to her bedroom. He heard the door slam. He had spoken to wound. He was still shaking from seeing the Saint Christopher, the size of a pea, catching the light between the boy's nails. In a moment's carelessness it might fall to the ground and roll out of sight where no one would ever find it again even if the whole room was turned upside-down.

Penny couldn't grasp how Jack suffered. She understood only that he who wanted her happiness considered the romance to be wrong. Time would prove its rightness. But she had no way of knowing what else time might do to her burning feelings. She was starting anew. That's what made her sing. There was nothing to remember except what dated from the day she met Rob, from the beginning of the new life she had not found at school up in town. With Rob a new world came within reach, as in their lovemaking – timid, exploratory, unconsummated – they danced into tomorrow, not hankering after the past.

Penny already had a woman's shrewdness. She understood her uncle's fears, and had her own plans too, for next year, and Leaving Honours, and beyond. Now there was a deeper plan. She wanted her love for Rob to reach maturity. She wanted to enjoy its evolution, its changes, its shaping of her world. That meant waiting.

From February Rob started to work long days on his father's property. Penny got her schoolbooks out and put them by her case. They didn't discuss the matter. One Saturday, a cloudy day that anticipated autumn, they were meandering among the rock pools in front of the shack – purposeless, motionless lovers, putting their fingers in anemones, plucking out crabs or white round pebbles – when Rob, whose thoughts were expressed crabwise, led up to the suggestion that Penny should not go back to school but should stay in the district, get engaged, wait for a year and then marry him.

His desire to be a man, his will for ownership (she knew) made him speak his plans, when she was still a virgin. He assumed things too easily, yet a pulse of warm satisfaction ran along her nerves.

'It's not that,' she said. 'You don't understand. I *want* to study. I *want* to become a lawyer. That's what I want to be. Not just a farmer's wife, even if the farmer is you.'

Rob stuck out his lip. He took her message obliquely. 'Is it anything to do with your uncle?' He clenched his fist.

'No, it's *me*. It's nothing to do with anyone else, it's just me. Please see that, Rob, or if you can't see, accept it anyway, that it's me, how I want my life to be. It doesn't get in the way of how I feel about you.'

'Bullshit. You'll be up in town. Out of reach. What am I supposed to do? Aren't you afraid I won't stick around?'

'If you don't, it will only be to spite me. If you don't stay around, good riddance.'

He hung his head, seeing that she was striking a bargain.

'Rob – ' She touched him, 'I know it's a hard test, but it's better for both of us.'

'I can't wait like that, not all the time. Without a promise. With no guarantee. It's not natural. It's not bloody fair.'

'Do what you like. If we do come back together, then

it will be real.'

'It's the end then. Is that what you're saying? You want to be free to go off with other people. Hell, I only asked you to marry me! Sorry I ever spoke.'

She stopped her stepping round pools and looked him in the face frankly and earnestly. Because she loved him, she would risk losing him.

'Wait,' she said, 'only wait. Wait.'

He had nothing to reply. He took her hand, squeezing it as a baby squeezes its mother's finger. On the cliff top the door banged as Jack Tregenza came out, shading his eyes to look for them. Penny saw and waved. Rob, squeezing her hand, made her turn seawards. That empty, tranquil, rippling space was where he would lose her, because he had no rope long enough to tie her to him across the distance she wanted to go.

'There's nothing out there, Pen. Nothing.'

He had hurt in his voice. She smiled, victoriously. It was the test. He had to let her go.

They crossed the sand to the base of the steps and climbed up together to where Uncle Jack stood planted on the verandah, watching, his arms firmly crossed. A week later Penny Tregenza put on her school uniform and caught the bus to Adelaide.

Later, pulling the plough, Rob Stewart began to wonder if he shouldn't go back to technical college.

Jack Tregenza ate his solitary meal and was pleased when, periodically, Rob called in as a matter of loyalty and asked for news of the girl.

# 3 • DRIFT, 1953

ONE WINTER, WHEN PENNY WAS turning eight, Jack came home from work and found a large car parked by the farmhouse. It shone sumptuously with the rounded corners of those days, the blackest thing in a scene of sandy rock, rust-stained tin and bright, wet grass. In the living room Penny sat dangling her legs from a straight-backed chair, animated as she talked to the lady who had come like a fairy godmother with lollies and a red smile. Deeper in the armchair was a robust man in a cardigan; and no sooner was Jack in the door than Bertha Cope came running, pretending to busy herself with tea.

'I told her you wouldn't be home for a bit, and she said she'd have a cup of tea and wait anyway,' apologized Bertha, the housekeeper who stayed on with Penny after school. It wasn't her place to decide what to do. 'Hello Vera,' she had said, and asked no more.

Jack was equally at a loss. He put up a barrier of stammering words as Vera rose to face him. A kiss would be too intimate, a handshake too formal.

'I wondered whose it could be,' he said finally, turning to take the man's grip. 'Nice car, Stan.'

'Since we were down this way,' explained Vera, 'we thought it would be silly not to call in.'

She invited attention in her spotted navy suit. The wide lapels of her cream silk shirt were folded back to expose her neck. Scarlet nails and lips set off her gold chains. And beneath Vera's grooming, fiery blood showed in her cheeks and big round hands. Her red hair waved off her face in a glossy crown that might have been natural. She showed no signs of wear and tear, no flagging spirits, as she held herself upright, her face a little flat, with too much attack in her eyes to put others or herself at ease.

'I'll make another pot,' said Bertha Cope, clearing out.

Jack fumbled. 'What a surprise. I never thought – ' It was up to him to declare the nature of the occasion.

'We've only dropped in for a cuppa, Jack.'

'Have you been talking to Penny?' He looked at the tongue-tied child, not at Vera.

'She's been telling us all sorts of stories, haven't you, darling?'

Penny smirked and swept her hair out of her eyes, tilting her head upwards in a gesture that made Vera redden. With pursed, flame-coloured lips she searched the girl's face for identity, and Penny's eyes danced anxiously before the peering adults. She grabbed a sweet from the bag Vera had given her and gobbled it disgustingly, mockingly, as she flopped against her chair back like a raggedy doll.

At the age of seven-and-three-quarters Penny had chubby arms, and legs like stuffed stockings. Her middle was a barrel of rippling energy and puppy fat that barely contained the exertions of everyday life and growth. Only her face had an adult's theatrical seriousness. She would frown and want to know everything. With her dolls and her invisible companions on the farm she would be a terrible know-all in turn. She was often alone.

Silky ginger hair played down her back, a bow tacked on somewhere for form's sake, and her skin was milky and freckled. She was healthy, strong and, more importantly, unafraid. Sometimes her placidity became a mood, sulky and in-turned like her young uncle Jack's; otherwise, as her school report said, she got on well with others and knew when to settle down. She was a most loving child, devoted to those who were kind to her and discriminating about those who weren't. Jack's steady, scarcely expressed love, and such regulars as Bertha Cope and Kath and Les Hocking made the days of her childhood still and warm, like the rich cream which had daily come to the top of the milk from Granny Irene's best cows.

Here was Vera come to inspect from the vantage point of her prime. Barely thirty, Vera Binns-that-was seemed to have known all the world – relative to the rustic peninsula of course. That was how she carried herself – Mrs Petchek now – wearing the rings and chains Stan had given her as proof. Stan's perfect incisor teeth flashed under his grained lip and Balkan moustache. Though not as tall as Vera, he was twice as broad, and strong as an ox. In winter his olive, sallow skin dreamed of heat and his eyes drooped bloodshot and yellow; he was an exile whose other world burned in the roots of his soul. The rest of the time, he was a lively wheeler-dealer whose eyes blazed with the different fire of the present. Stan Petchek was a Dalmatian fisherman who had made good, Vera the meaty mermaid who wore his glittering seaweed jewellery.

'Howsa going, Jack?' His English hadn't changed. Still the jolly fragments of interrogation, the boasts. 'We jus' bought a new boat – big one – she'sa beautiful – go right across to New Zealand for the tuna – freeze them on the boat. For the cans. All fish for the cans all round the world.'

'How are the boys?' asked Jack. Stan's cheeks dimpled paternally. 'They're nice-looking kids.'

'Eddie's six and Tony's five,' informed Vera. 'Both at school now, for heaven's sake. Little toughies like their old man. Little Tony's the character. He's got to fend for himself against Eddy and he takes some watching. Gee that little kid makes me laugh. All that swagger, only five years old.'

'Boys are pathetic,' proclaimed Penny. She had arrived at the conviction with her two best girlfriends from school. 'I bet they pull girls' hair and bite their legs.'

'Hoo,' Stan hooted, 'in one year or two, you see!'

'They need a lady like you, Penny, to teach them some manners,' said Vera. 'Isn't she a terrific little person, Jack? She's going to be a real beauty.'

The child's face was blank and docile. What else could she do? She didn't like being talked about in that way. Saying nothing, Jack put his hand on the nape of the girl's neck, and Penny understood.

When the second pot of tea was finished and they had chatted long enough, Vera rose to go, as good as her word. 'Come on – ' She looped her arm round Stan's, who was surprised they weren't staying for dinner. Vera had a sense of procedure that Jack found ominous. She concealed her purpose, playing fair. On the way to the car, she got Jack aside and asked him for a quick tour of the garden. The chilly evening didn't deter her, and when they were behind the orange trees against the railing of the old fence to the paddocks, years and politeness were stripped away.

'You're doing a good job, Jack. No one can say you're not. But the easy part's behind you. I didn't mention a thing to the kid, because I didn't want to confuse her. Lord knows what stories you've told! She seems pretty agitated to me and will probably ask a few questions when I've gone. It's up to you, Jack. Tell her what you like and I'll go along with it for the time being. Only promise me that you'll come if you ever need help, that you won't be too bloody proud. I'm not saying I wouldn't have done exactly the same if I had my time over. It's worked out, Jack. Better than some other things might have done. Anyway,' with decisive fingerwork she flattened her lapels and stared for a moment at the glum paddock, 'Stan'll be wondering where we've got to.'

The cold air and her fast talking made Vera breathless. Settled now, she could afford to rekindle her maternal spirit. Or was it the cauterized feelings of years before exacting their revenge? Jack imagined Vera at the mercy of her passions, nothing more. He was sure no good would come of it, and wanted the visit over. As they waved goodbye he held tight to Penny's hand, thinking what to tell her.

'Vera's done well for herself,' said Bertha who had stayed late out of curiosity. Tomorrow all Wooka would know. 'She's always been a fine-looking woman. I bet Stan doesn't put up with any nonsense from her. I've done an hour extra today, Jack, so I'll be a bit late in the morning if you don't mind.' Bundled up in a winter coat with a bag under her arm, Bertha Cope had on her pious leaving look, guessing that Jack was in a fix over the visitor.

Afterwards, he sat moodily over his meal, prodding his food about the plate as he always told Penny not to do. She didn't ask any questions to make it easier. She ate in a hurry. Jack waited, unable to define a situation which until then he had let be. Which had worked, as days and years passed. Now . . . . The girl ran from the table, leaving her uncle's thoughts uncommunicated. She sometimes thought of the fine ladies of Adelaide, and here had been one in the room, smelling, shining, wearing clothes that couldn't be got dirty. When would the lady come again so they could have a party? Would she be there for Christmas? A doll heard Penny's news, whispered on the floor of the bedroom – what the lady would say, what the lady would do, how the lady would act in her best ball gown.

A couple of days later, by the regular arrangement, Kath Hocking picked Penny up from school and took her home. The Hockings' was home away from home, where there were three children to play with, and Jack could call in after work for a drink with Les, the Town Clerk. Kath would have mothered the whole district if she'd been allowed. On this particular day Jack came early, before Les was home, and leaned against the bench talking to Kath with his arms folded. She had roses in her wide cheeks and thick black hair crudely permed. Her hips were too large for the kitchen, but her busy hands were nimble, as delicate as her dark alert eyes. A true countrywoman dedicated to health and continuance, Kath was always on the lookout for remedies. Her baking and bottling, her kind offers, her committees, her labouring dawn-to-dusk were all part of a mammoth contribution that in her opinion was scarcely more than the widow's mite. 'Lord give us strength,' she pleaded. And He did.

'Vera's turned up.'

Without facing him – she held a great oven dish between baking mitts – she said, 'So I hear. Lord give us strength.'

'Trouble, you think?'

'Vera's Vera. What did she want?'

'Nothing. But she'll be back.'

'P'r'aps not. P'r'aps it was a whim and you've frightened her off.'

'I wasn't very frightening, Kath. Besides, she seemed to take a liking to Penny.'

'Not surprising.'

'The truth is, Kath, I wonder if Penny mightn't be better off with Vera now. She's not a bad woman. She's got a family home and Stan's obviously made a packet. He's driving a Rover.'

'So I hear. Did you ever? Flash Stan!'

'Penny would have opportunities up in Adelaide, education-wise and so forth. There are things I can't give her. I'm only one man.'

'I'm hearing things, Jack Tregenza! What's got into you, talking like this? She's got you frightened, has she? You're not seriously going to sit on your backside and hand little Penny over to Vera Binns. Who are you fooling? When you're doing the best possible job – '

'Is that good enough?' blurted Jack.

'You're doing a bloody marvellous job! At first – well, you didn't know what you were letting yourself in for – that's why I offered, and I'm still here as far as that goes, Jack, you know that. Between us we can give that kid a thousand-times-better upbringing than Vera Binns with ten wop millionaires.'

'Maybe,' said Jack mournfully.

'No question,' she continued. 'You reckon that Vera is a decent woman? Well, far be it from me to be uncharitable, but no decent woman would have snuck in like that to the poor little kid. You weren't even home according to Bertha. Vera's a stirrer. The woman can't help herself.'

'You never liked her. Never forgiven her?'

'I hold no grudges. Things have worked out, Jack. The past is the past, over and done with as far as I'm concerned. But me like Vera Binns – *no*.'

'I don't want her stirring up painful feelings for Penny. That's hard.'

'We'd all be better off if she'd never come. She did come. That's typical. She'll be back. You just have to find a way of living with it. Poor soul!'

'Who, Penny?'

'Vera! The guilt that woman must feel! If she lets herself. It must be eating her heart away. Bertha reckoned she looked pretty swish.'

'If you'd seen Vera's expression – Even Penny knew something. Doesn't that give her the right?'

'There's nothing sacred about it, giving birth. It just happens, and a fine thing, too, for the most part. But Vera hasn't loved that kid. You've been devoted. Think of your own mother – Irene lived for that kid till her dying day. She'd turn in her grave if you went and handed her over now. You'd want your head read.'

'Blood is thicker than water. I can't stand in the way of that.'

'Don't dress it up, Jack. Vera has a legal right. You know that as well as I do. You wouldn't stand a chance in court. That's why Irene never tried – better let sleeping dogs lie. That's why you never did anything about becoming her guardian yourself. You were always afraid that Vera might come back one day, and now she has come back, and you're going to hang on, Jack Tregenza, for all you're bloody well worth. Only stop doubting yourself.'

Kath was stern. Afterwards she comforted him with a hearty meal, for all her family, and Jack, and Penny, sitting round the table. At the end Jack gave Kath a hug of gratitude and laid Penny, sleeping in a blanket, on the back seat of the car. He trundled home warm and humming. Would he tell Penny? She'd never forgive him if he didn't. But it would change everything, and he couldn't do that.

The same August that Vera came back one of the school children brought a nautilus shell to show his class, a small specimen, quite undamaged. As the teacher tenderly handled it, the children marvelled at how fragile the shell was. Some had seen the nautilus before in pride of place on a mantelpiece or nestled in cotton wool in a shell box, or as a pockmarked fragment that a parent ruefully picked up off a beach. But this specimen was newly washed up, newly found. The children were often told the tale that the nautilus comes sailing in, if the winter is right, once every seven years. Here was the first proof that they were again returning. For the children in Penny Tregenza's class it was the first time they had seen the story come true. She told her uncle Jack that evening, and he said he knew the best place for them. He promised to take her there when the conditions were right.

For a fortnight there was heavy rain, the sea was high and Jack said that no nautilus would reach the shore intact. Every day a brisk wind bent the trees and herded sheep into corners, and by mid-morning the sluggish masses of cloud gathered into diabolic fortresses that opened their ports and poured down on the earth. You went to sleep with rain pounding, and under darkness the storm renewed and whipped in off the sea. At last, however, it stopped, and the sky stayed silver bright till noontime.

It was a Sunday, and Jack said, 'Let's rug up and go.'

The track to his special place followed the ragged coastline through sheets of lying water and brassy bright grass blotched with trees. To seaward the crumbly biscuit rock had a green-gold burnish of lichen and weed. Exhausted after the storm, the sea was veiled by greasy winter blackness that made it alien and docile now in the windless conditions. The thin, pale sky was white where the sun lay buried in it. Almost overgrown, the track veered through low spiky scrub and weather-eaten limestone to the outreach of the bluff. Surfers used the track in summer, and Jack took it knowingly, though high grass scraped the belly of his car. The land rose to a headland where nothing obstructed the view in either direction. There was the sea, meeting the shore with the merest diplomatic offering of white froth, offshore vastly unperturbed. The track went down the side of the bluff and dissolved between trees and dunes. When the wheels started to spin, Jack said they would get out and walk.

There was no sand when they got to the beach. The shore and the water were black, and the sand was covered with black weed. The lapping water was as thick with weed as the stewed dregs of tea in a pot. It was a sight so strange as to make you laugh.

There were short, flat purple-olive strips of weed, black and speckled when dry, rolled up on the shore like cuttings from a great marine mowing. They lay in an unbroken mattress, half on the sand, half in the water, so it was impossible to tell where the sea started except that, as the waves rose and fell, part of the mattress moved too, until at the seamost edge it began to fray, or turn into a black prickly suspension stretched in the distance like the pelt of a huge drowned beast.

Jack grinned broadly. The sight was better than he expected. 'Gee!' gasped Penny before she ran at the weed, on to it, into it, giggling madly, sunk up to her chest in it. 'It's warm, Jack!' she yelled, amazed.

'Yep.'

'It's really hot.'

'It insulates. It's slowly combusting. Be careful, though. You'd be better off if you stripped down to your bloomers for when you fall in.'

'Yow-ee!'

The weed was piled so thickly it formed a raft for Penny's weight. She could wade through it and lie on a thick bit and not get wet, even where water was underneath. If she made a false move she would fall through into the slimy soup. Even that was strangely warm. Daubed from head to foot in black sticky weed, she was wild with joy.

Jack jiggled his way into the rubber goloshes he wore to net fish – great baggy rubber overalls that covered him to the waist. He walked like a spaceman, slowly, clumsily, through the warm mass of weed.

'Hey, Pen,' he called, 'keep a lookout for any sharp things. There'll be shells – they could be nautilus.'

Jack knew that the little cove filled with weed whenever the nautilus came, and the weed acted as protection to stop the shells bashing against rocks or beach as they came in. The weed caught the shells unharmed, but you had to find them without breaking them yourself, buried deep in the waves of weed.

'Jack!' sung out Penny – and a huge ball of seaweed hit him in the face, sprayed inside his overalls, was rank on his lips. He made to charge at Penny, but his legs stuck in the weed and he tumbled forward. She squealed with glee.

'You'll be sorry,' he shouted.

'*You'll* be sorry,' she returned as another ball of weed cometed into his face.

Jack watched acutely for white angles in the black weed. He had a good eye, and presently found a piece of shell as big as his hand. Its surface had the regular pinched pattern of miniature scalloping, the broken side of a huge nautilus, a parachute with a razor-sharp edge. Jack waved it in the air as a sign.

'Promise you won't push me in the seaweed! Promise!' she called.

'I promise.'

She came curiously to examine the token of what they were seeking. It would be pure luck if they found one, as they worked hard sifting the weed in search of a shell that might not exist or might crack in your hands as you reached for it. In the process Penny unearthed driftwood, frilly cockles, conches, bottles and bleached plastic containers. Jack was moved watching her dogged search. She had become a sea baby with black weed tagged to her gold hair and dark wet stains on her white bloomers and skin.

The sea shone lead-dull as the sun went lower in the wintry sky. The water rose around the tumbled rocks at the base of the bluff. They had found nothing when Jack, staring crankily, wearily at the sea, saw a small white corner out far.

'What's that?' he called to Penny. 'Over there?'

Waist-high in weed, her nuggety body turned where he pointed. Her hand was to her eyes, like a skipper. 'Don't know,' she said. 'Is it one?'

'Might be a cuttlefish.'

'A message in a bottle.'

He grinned blankly as he stared at the sharp-looking thing in the sea. Penny went back to her absorbed search, her game of fantasy in the playground of sea-wrack.

When he was certain, he shouted, 'It's a nautilus.' From a distance, as they watched, the shell became unequivocal.

To see one arrive was rare, carried by winds and currents towards the shore, and it absorbed Jack and Penny's gaze as it moved slowly, steadily towards them, until quite by chance Penny looked beyond.

'There's another one! Behind!'

'And another one! There's three.' In a small convoy the

nautilus sailed towards the shore, bobbing, sometimes disappearing, their white quarter-circle prows glowing against the dark sea.

Jack and Penny waded into the suspension of weed that the shells would have to negotiate. Penny was up to her shoulders in the icy sea water, no longer warmed by the weed's blanket, and the water was about to spill inside Jack's rubber pants. They held out their arms longingly, hopelessly – the shells were as far away as ever, drifting in the mild shoreward current across the windless surface of the ocean.

'How can we get them?' asked Penny.

'We'll just have to wait.'

'How long will it take?'

'We'll find out, won't we? We might as well go back on dry land and wait, eh, before we freeze to death?'

The light was fading and the shells' journey was taking them away from the centre of the beach towards the rocks beneath the bluff. There was little chance they would shatter there, in the masses of weed, but every chance that they would be embedded in weed among rocks where it was too deep and dangerous to reprieve them.

'Patience,' said Jack. 'Wait and see. Why don't we light a fire?'

The dry-enough sticks they found smoked and caught, burned for a bit and went out, and all the paper was gone. Time had passed and the shells, harder now to see, came closer in the darkness, curving away from the rocks towards the midpoint of the cove where their travel slowed as they entered the thickets of weed. It was freezing on the shore.

Jack spoke decisively. 'The best bet is to swim out and get them.'

'It's too dark. How will you find them? You'll freeze!'

'You stand as far out as you can and direct me, okay?'

She was as miserable as a puppy as Jack took off his thick clothes. Yet he moved easily through the weed with his young man's strength and she was encouraged to follow behind. He waded as far as possible and began a quiet breast-stroke. Penny bounced nervously on her tiptoes. She could see his head.

'Just in front of you,' she yelled into space. But he wouldn't hear. He couldn't see a thing, just kept on swimming. The water was over his depth.

'Over a bit. Just in front. Over a bit,' she shouted. Her eyes ached for his splashing head and the white shells in the gloom.

He reached the first, biggest shell and held it up in the air, as light and frail as air itself. He might have crushed it with his grip. He trod water, circling, losing sense for a moment where the shore was. He sighted another shell and, protecting the big one against his chest, swam sidestroke towards it. The second shell was smaller and he nestled it in his underpants. There remained one more.

He was too tired to search properly in the dark. He stayed feebly moving his legs in a single spot. What foolhardiness! It was too late, and there was all the shoreward swim to manage. In that instant, panic insinuated its tentacles round his working legs. And in the same instant the third nautilus bumped lightly against his head, and he cupped his hands round it as a gift.

'Penny', he called. 'Pen-ny!' He needed her direction.

'Jack, Ja-ack!' High and dim. An overstrained, rhythmic machine, his body turned towards the shore. At last the weed began to thicken, and gave him support. He carved a way through, until it became a solid mattress, and Penny was there, holding her hands out for the shells.

He brayed exultantly. 'A good hot bath for both of us! A good fire and a good feed!'

She walked close behind him to the car.

On inspection, the three shells proved flawless, descending in size.

They were Penny's pride when she took them to school on Monday. The teacher found the page in the shell book from the South Australian Museum, and Penny copied out the strange words carefully.

*Paper Nautilus Argonauta nodosa Solander 1786 Argonaut. Parchment-like, white, dark brown on the earlier knobs of the keel. Not a true shell, but the egg-nest of an octopus-like animal. Ocean beaches. 7 inches. Argonautidae.*

They were precious and beautiful.

In spring Vera and Stan Petchek returned again and installed themselves in the Wooka pub. Rumour had it they were investigating sites for a holiday house. Jack knew better. They had come for Penny's birthday, and he was obliged to ask them to the party. He had planned nothing special, a birthday dinner with Bertha Cope's roast lamb, a cake, and all the Hockings attending. If he asked Vera too, it would condone her claim, yet how could he not? To refuse would force a challenge. He could not deny her. When he rang the hotel Vera sounded as if the thought had never crossed her mind. What a delightful idea! How sweet!

The same day, closing the office early, Jack met Penny after school. They sat together in the front seat as she waited stiffly for the man to explain what was amiss. Her new riding boots, Jack's present, the colour of rosewood, knocked against each other. To adopt an air of indifference was Penny's way of preparing for bad news. When something bad happened, she always acted airily, as if to confirm her independence. That pretence took all her young strength of character.

Jack said nothing until they were home together in the kitchen.

'You remember that lady Vera who came and saw us that time? She was a nice lady. You wanted to know when she was coming back. She's coming back tomorrow. She's coming for your birthday.'

'Is she?' Penny didn't smile.

'Penny, listen. When Granny Irene died and you came to live with me – you remember that?'

'I walked all the way to you in the dark,' she bragged.

'You were four years old. We never thought you would stay with me forever, did we? After all I'm not your father. You know that, don't you?'

'You're Jack.'

'I'm your Uncle Jack. I'm Granny Irene's other son. Your Granny Irene wasn't your mother, either, though she loved you like a mother. You know she was your grandmother, don't you?'

The hurt spread across Penny's face, though she didn't flinch. The memory of her Granny Irene lived within her as all she knew of mother love. In silence she protested against the truth Jack was forcing on her.

'Your father was my brother Peter. Granny Irene's son. He was a wonderful man. He would be so proud to see you now – and you can be proud of him. He would be the best father to you, if he was here. Only he died in the war. Granny Irene used to talk to you about him. Do you remember? He loved your real mother too. They were meant for each other, they were meant to have you. But it was very difficult for your mother without Peter. She knew it was better if you went to live with Granny Irene. It hurt her very much to give you up, but she had no choice. So she left you here in Wooka and went far away, to Adelaide, to start a new life and never come back. That lady is Vera.'

'I know,' said Penny with greedy pleasure. 'I know.'

'Who told you?'

'I know I know I know. She's come to give me presents and take me away to Adelaide. I know. My mother is rich and beautiful and she wants me.' Penny spoke with full drama. 'But I'm staying with you, Uncle Jack.'

Still he did the decent thing. 'Don't you want to be with your mother?'

Penny would say not another word on the subject.

At least there were children at the birthday meal – six in all with the two Petchek boys – running around raucously in violent play while the parents stood like outsize umpires to protect the interests of their own without too obviously taking sides. Comparative statistics – ages and achievements – were bandied about. Sidelong, all eyes were on Vera, who showed off her russet wool with a perfect smile.

The Hockings had any amount of compassion at the ready. They would see whether Vera had set herself apart or was one of them, and they would judge. Their acquaintance with Vera's people over the generations did nothing to soften their practical, conditional morality.

Vera and Kath held identical glasses of sherry, side by side. Kath had no intention of moving away, though Vera made her feel ungainly, even if proud. If she was big at the hips, and fatter than suited her delicate hands, and dressed with an assemblage of colour, not elegance, if her hair was curled in country fashion and her features righteous, at least she was more honest than Vera, who had arrived at her present poise by smoothing away the sharper edges of her story. To have Stan there was good. Whatever else Vera did, Stan was still the man who had handled mountains of silver, oily fish, his hair as glossy as sardines. Vera had hurt Kath. But Kath's trump was that Vera would never know what cross-grained strength that hurt of years ago had given to Kath's life. To Vera, Kath was simply another of the women who stayed on in the district, bovine with a difficult streak. She did not know how Kath's pain, her thwarting, had been turned into a capital asset.

Kath watched for traces of maternal feeling between Vera and Penny. She had an excellent eye for such things, and had set Les to watch too. Squeezed in at the eating table, Vera was ladylike. Stan was magnificent in his acceptance of all the food and drink and human presence, one son squirming in the crook of his elbow, one of

Bertha's fishpaste shapes on his tongue, and a forkful of meat in the other hand. Jack had carved the home-killed leg to the bone.

'Nothing like it,' said Stan. The flavoursome lamb of Australia had always reminded him of his Dalmatian home when nothing else could save him.

Amongst the mealtime business of elbowing and clattering, reaching wide to cut up food for kids or pass what one person has neglected to another who loves it, there was no chance for serious talk. A boy again, Jack closed his drunken eyes on the threat of the occasion. He couldn't defend Penny, or himself, except by trusting with blind faith to the merry moment. So he joined in Stan Petchek and Les Hocking's hearty enjoyment, leaving the rest to the women – of whom the birthday girl was one.

Afterwards they settled in chairs or perched around the sides of the living room, with Jack waiting at the light switch for Bertha to bring in the pink-and-white cake. Eight candles bloomed suddenly from the swirling shadows of the room's perimeter and the cake tilted down in reach of Penny, who brooded like an ancient sorceress as she breathed in for an exaggerated puff – and blew out all eight. Amid clapping and cheers Jack turned on the light, and the pearl-handled knife was put between Penny's fingers.

'Make a wish! A wish!'

The knife sliced to the platter beneath.

As they sang, Vera refrained from joining in. She stood illuminated beside the standard lamp with an expression of good humour, detached from the general enchantment. She approved – as if the scene continued only by her dispensation. Assuming Vera's pose to be a version of envy, Kath took extra pleasure in going forward with a parcel loosely wrapped in crumpled paper.

'Happy birthday, darling!'

A stripy beach towel unrolled into Penny's hands – a splash of summer; then came a neat package of talc and perfumed soap from Bertha Cope. Jack's present – the riding boots she had always needed – had been worn to school that day. Now they stood shining on display beside the fireplace.

Vera touched Stan's arm to send him to the car. While he was gone she kicked aside the wrapping paper to clear a space on the carpet. She looked almost too grand. The others were shocked when she dropped to her knees in front of Penny and took the child's hands. With Vera kneeling, the woman and the girl were the same height. No words were needed to point the resemblance. The mother's auburn was only the mature version of the daughter's ginger-gold, swept back off the same high forehead. Vera's sense of theatre was precise. No one could make a sound, as the one fact they wished to deny was demonstrated so amply.

In the silence Vera began, 'Since today is your birthday, and a special occasion, I have something very special to tell you, in front of all our friends.' She did not for a flicker shift her gaze from the child whose hands she held; yet true to the actor's art, all her responsiveness was to the onlookers. 'What I have to tell you, darling, is very precious. I am your mother. Yes, your mother has come back to you after all these years, and it is I. This is your birthday. I remember this day, eight years ago exactly, when you were born. I remember it better than anyone. Isn't it lovely that we can be together again? You're my beautiful little girl, and Jack's looked after you so well for me all these years. Give me a hug, darling.'

For Vera to make that speech took guts – not because of the encircling faces of the adults, aghast, but because of Penny who stared at the lady with piercing suspicion. As Vera spoke, Penny gradually leaned away from her, curving inwards, tucking her chin into her chest as she peered from under frowning brows – a movement of reluctance, denial. She crossed her arms round her body to protect herself, resisting to the utmost any compulsion to fall helplessly against this mother's breast. In the end Vera had to seize her. When this happened Penny collapsed, wrapped round the woman like a cub. But she didn't keep her eyes buried in Vera's wool for long. She quickly found Uncle Jack among the staring faces, to show him. As a child with no say in the outcome, the best she could do was rise to the occasion. She hugged the woman like a long-lost child hugging its mother. It was all a great act.

Wriggling out of Vera's embrace she said, 'I already know you're my mother. Everybody knows that.'

'Do they?' Vera was unperturbed. She waved for Stan to deposit the enormous carton he had jostled in from outside. As the errand boy Stan was happier, not having expected, from Vera's subtleties, such an eruption of drama. He hoped his sons wouldn't remember. He was too much a fisherman to have the fixed ideas and self-love of land people. To forget, to let things wash away, was always better. He demanded that of his wife too, usually. Her past was inland as far as he was concerned, left behind from the day he had called at that particular port and swept her off elsewhere. So he believed, and would be patient now till the tide turned again.

The unpacked present was a thing of miraculous and exact craftsmanship, a charming miniature French chateau with three storeys and a lifting roof and every room exquisitely furnished: with little people in their respective outfits, little copper vessels below stairs in the kitchen with rubicund scullery maids. Above, in an entrance hall lined with gilt mirrors and postage-stamp portraits, stood a pair of porters acting as doorstops, and in the drawing room a suite of plush-and-gilt Louis Quatorze chairs. The diminutive denizens of this beau monde were upstairs adorning or undoing themselves, the gentleman laid erect as a tiny corpse on a chintz matchbox bed, while next door his lady, or kept woman, sat bewigged in a boudoir tizz before a vanity mirror and a wobbling servant with a not-quite-to-scale Sèvres chamberpot.

Hélas! The lacquer gleamed so brightly that it mocked the ordinary room where the real people gathered, bending to peer into the glinting world of satin, felt and toymanship. Everything was in its place – the little people glued to the spot – and Vera as she held back the lid for the light assumed a position no less secure, and much loftier, in relation to the perfect model house and the scheme of things generally. The house had been to her design so that Penny should know the dream of something else, and could not fail to captivate, as Vera, chirping like a bird, took the child through every chamber. The gift was a calculated bribe, Penny knew, but at eight she was too sensible not to admire it.

Kath's colour was high. As soon as Vera rose to her feet she hissed, 'You know how to choose your moment, Vera! You might have been more considerate – in the middle of a kid's birthday party like that. You might have consulted someone.'

'Kath, no – ' said Jack. 'Leave it. It's Penny's birthday.'

'I wanted Penny to know,' – there was something in Vera's throat – 'to know how things really are. The knowledge can't hurt.'

'The knowledge *can* hurt, Vera,' said Kath definitively. 'Did you think of that?'

'Please, not now,' Jack begged.

Voices were not yet raised. The hoarse stage whispers pushed the explosion down into rancour. On the napes of necks, hairs were charged.

'Penny must know the truth if ever she wants to make up her own mind.'

'About what, Vera?'

'You're all so bloody afraid of me. Don't be, Kath. I don't want anything except to help.'

'That's enough for tonight,' said Jack. It was his house. 'Let's cut the cake into pieces and everyone can take a bit home.'

Jack feared more than anything that he would lose Penny. Briskly, desperately, he directed the remainder of the evening back towards chitchat and gaiety. His face was colourless all the while, as he too became the blank child who knows only how to accommodate. He knew of old what it was like to be cheated and powerless, to lose the love you had dared to hope was the permanent face of the world's goodness. There was no point putting up another fight.

After Vera and Stan had gone with their boys, and Bertha had tidied up, Kath stayed and ranted. Jack couldn't listen. He let Kath put Penny to bed and slumped in the armchair, preferring Les Hocking's hefty scotch.

'Vera's gone and done it now,' said Les.

'What's done is done,' said Jack.

'Maybe. Cheers.'

In the dark house, later, Jack heard Penny's voice calling small and high, the familiar call, its urgency muted by the sure faith that an answer would come.

'Ja-ack!'

He went and sat on her bed in the darkness.

'I can't get to sleep.'

It was the usual pretext, and he gave the usual response.

'Sh. I'll tuck you in.'

In their ritual he went round the bed, tightly tucking her in.

'Go to sleep now.'

'Is my mother coming back again tomorrow?'

'I don't know. Probably. Don't worry about it, my darling.'

'I'm not worried, Uncle Jack. Night-night.'

She rolled over under the blankets.

'Night,' he said, dismissed. Her mind was strange and strong; he must trust to that.

A conversation took place the following day behind the frosted glass partition of Jack's office in the stock and station agency. The space outside the partition was filled with farm machinery painted bright as toys, and stacked with chemicals in drums and boxes, sprays, fertilizers and dips. On this day it made a no-man's-land, because once Vera Binns was seen to enter and cross the place to where Jack sat, no one else would go in until she came out again. In any case Stan's Rover was parked in the street, with Stan in the front seat and the car door open letting the sun on his thighs while he perused the newspaper. The boys were in the back. They were a guard outside until Vera's business was done.

Vera was determined to keep a conversational tone. She was not, however, offered a seat. Instead Jack stood on the other side of the neat bare-ish desk with wire baskets in each corner for IN and OUT. He knew why she had come and did not want to hear, because there was no stopping her anyway. Best keep it to a brief announcement. But Vera this time was not direct. She began by thanking him, on behalf of all the Petcheks, for the marvellous birthday occasion. Her cheeks were plump and rosy as she smiled, to make Jack smile and share a decent recognition that there were things to be enjoyed no matter what. That had to be the basis. People who refused jollity were not to be bothered with, people who introduced too many complications and implied judgement with their downturned mouths. That was Vera's position.

In any case Jack had always been a misery britches. He sank down into sorrow whenever his dreamy sense of things was unsettled. Vera wasn't going to give him a chance for that, even as she watched him shrink inside his clothes like a snail. With highlights round the eyes and an exuberant frock, she insisted on glowing brightly.

'You must have enjoyed yourself,' said Jack glumly.

'Don't sound so accusing,' she laughed. 'We all had a good time, didn't we? I bet Penny did. A night to remember!'

'It was that.' Jack was unable to resist feeling forlorn.

'Why don't you just say what your purpose is, Vera. You have a perfect right. I don't accuse. No point in that.'

She opened her handbag and fiddled for cigarettes. 'I was hoping we could have a little chat. Do you mind if I sit down?' she said. It was hopeless to try and smoke on her feet.

'Sorry, I didn't mean to be rude.' Even his politeness was a way of yielding. He curled and twisted himself into the recesses of his cushioned desk chair.

Cocking her head to assess him, she began, 'You know, you haven't changed a bit. You always shrank away from me. When you were cornered and couldn't shrink any further you always used to put on that same downcast face. I got you wrong when I thought I could make it better for you. That's never what you wanted.'

'Wouldn't you be downcast?' When his voice reached the bitter rut of sarcasm, there was nowhere else to go. 'You shouldn't've done that last night,' he blurted. 'What if she hadn't known?'

'But she did know.'

'Did you have to go and make such a scene of it? There are other ways of doing a thing like that.'

'I haven't had previous experience,' replied Vera in a high, scornful tone, before her glance dropped.

'You should have thought, before you came meddling.'

'My own daughter . . .'

'You should have thought.' Jack seemed stupid, repeating himself, incapable of understanding, as if eyes and ears and nostrils and mouth were filled with sand. Vera re-crossed her legs impatiently.

'On the contrary – ' She insisted on her logic, 'I gave it a great deal of thought. I decided I had to let her know who I was . . . and where . . . I had to let Penny know that her mother exists. I had to put myself within her reach. That is something between her and me. She has to know the bond exists – special and private – and everyone else has to feel that too, even if it's bloody uncomfortable for them.'

Vera's granite facts were as grey as Jack's self-pity.

'If you cared about Penny, couldn't you have consulted me? You couldn't know how much she's wanted you in the past — how much she's imagined a mother — when the questions were asked — when you didn't happen to be here — '

'Don't, Jack.'

'She woke up expecting again today.'

'She doesn't reject me like the rest of you.'

'You just come barging in, Vera. As I say, you have the perfect right. Only there's no mercy in it.'

Jack's crusty face threatened to crack into tears, and Vera quickened with the hot anger of love she must hold down. The man would never understand.

'There was a pitifully small portion of mercy for myself, that's all. A wretched bit.' She spoke in a voice that steadied all emotion, blaming him. 'Let me explain it to you, Jack, since the closest you can come is to talk about my perfect right. In the world where I live, and where you refuse to live, Jack Tregenza, there are no *rights*. There is only the cruelty of what happens. In that world it is paramount to live as best you can. Happiness, that's all that matters. Why? Because happiness is the easiest thing to lose on account of some imaginary principle.'

Jack frowned, in deepening perplexity, wondering where Vera got the energy for her strange words. His chair swivelled left and right beneath him.

'You judge me because I left the baby. You judge me because Stan has given me what I want. Comfort, pride, respectability, *love* by all its names — but at bottom what he gave me was *pleasure*. The creature needs that just as she needs food and drink. He gave it — no, he forced it on me like a true healer when I was expected to live on endless hope, like the mallee roots that old Irene was always going on about in her grieving: good to keep the stove going all night, once they were thoroughly dried out. Hopeless it was, starving *I* was – Stan wouldn't have let me refuse what he offered. Nor was I such a fool. He has his honour. That won't be ruffled. I can understand that, after the way this town has treated me. "Respectable" is a word which means something. It means he can say his kids are his own. Sorry I have to say it to you like this, Jack. I'm not taking Penny with me. I decided that before all this started. My own daughter. I just hoped she was in good hands. She couldn't be in better hands. You'd have made a good dad.'

He could not bring himself to sit forwards in his chair. Because Vera, he considered, cared only for satisfaction, he had no confidence that she did not care to take Penny.

'I made the decision, for Stan's sake and my own. But I couldn't bear a complete separation, to forget completely – '

'You've forgotten for seven years.'

'Provisionally, as it turned out. Forgetting is slow. Remembering gets stronger and demands to be satisfied. I gave myself one occasion to put myself in Penny's life so neither of us would ever forget. It's not just myself I want her to remember, either, but the larger world – pleasure, excitement, *satisfaction*. When she wishes there was something else, I want her to come to me.'

'Do you think I don't want that for her?'

'You do, but not the pain. You would never upset her enough to make her fight for the things she needs. You're a good father, like I said.'

Vera's power lay not in the blood bond of motherhood, but in the bewitching intuition she drew from her experience of the world. She knew all about desire and satisfaction, moving on, reaching for, getting and forgetting. Those were things she wanted for Penny. That was her bequest.

'If you're leaving Penny, if that's what you're doing, I can only say I'm grateful. I could never give her up if the child was mine.'

'That's it, Jack. If you gave her up, she wouldn't be yours any more. I can go away and she's more mine than ever.'

Jack stood up, at attention, like a soldier, in response to the old feeling of facing the worst thing he could ever know. He said to Vera, 'It's horrible.'

'It's hard. I've made the decision, but I can't leave without having her see me one more time.'

Vera regretted those words. She had presented her structures of compromise as solid land masses; yet the gain and loss turned out again as curly and unsupportive as the sea. She was not at all sure, as she left, what she had told Jack or what he might have seen.

His last question was almost blank, as if she had never spoken.

'If she wants to go with you, will you take her?'

He might have been interceding, on the child's behalf.

'Do you trust her that much?'

The man was astonishing – a fool. Vera didn't bother to wait for his answer.

For a moment Jack mused on sacrifice. He thought he knew the animal inside out.

Sacrifice? She had suited herself – and Jack was terrifically relieved.

Knowing each farmhouse, each inhabitant, each turning of the road, the piles of limestone, the rises where you could see the sea, Penny was not frightened when she had to walk home from school. The long dirt road cut through wide vistas of lush new grass, under a bright spring sky scattered with fluffy pillows of cloud. She was like any other schoolgirl, hair in pigtails, skirt too long, socks down, trailing a small brown case. If anyone came in sight, she knew who they were. If a car came, going her way, they would give her a lift. But the large black car that shot past did not notice her in its churned-up dust.

Stan at the wheel was arguing with Vera. The holiday was over, he said, wanting to get home. Indulgence was among the things he prided himself on giving her. He had been tickled by the curiosity that brought her back to the peninsula all of a sudden, for a lark. But enough was enough. Too much and it got silly. Stan hated anything that might make him a buffoon.

'Keep it brief,' he said, 'if we must go there at all. There'll be other trips. We've been round enough this time. I don't like sneakin' about, not when Jack's not home.'

'Penny's expecting me. Jack knows that. We can't leave without saying goodbye, pet.'

The Petchek boys were brawling in the back. They were on Stan's side, not liking the stiff way their mother held her neck as she looked down the road without bothering to turn and tick them off. Their own napes would bristle like Stan's one day.

Stan turned up Jack's drive and parked carelessly at the front of the house. Vera was already crossing the lawn when Bertha Cope came out expecting the worst. Vera was quite subdued as she asked to see the child, and Bertha's obstructive reply only spurred her to march forward. If the child was not there, she would wait, with renewed determination or need. 'Tea,' Bertha offered, and made sure that Stan and the boys came slouching in from the car. They were grumpy, settled awkwardly in the livingroom that had been swept bare of the previous evening's party. A pale, cold, mercuric light chastened the springy sagging chairs, as Bertha fussed – her own chance for theatre now – quite absurdly with the teaset.

When Penny trudged up the drive she recognized the car slewed across the front lawn. She crossed the yard to the back door and waved at Bertha through the kitchen window. Bertha was signalling something, evidently in a flap, and hurried outside, wiping her hands on her apron so she could smooth down Penny's hair and pullover.

'Vera's inside,' clucked Bertha, exposing the tip of her tongue, 'can't keep Vera waiting.' The woman's hands were fixing and shaping Penny all over.

Penny waved her arms like a windmill to get Bertha off, her feet rooted to the ground. Bertha yanked; and Penny yanked in resistance.

'I don't want to see her!'

'You've got to see her – after the dolls' house she gave you.'

'I'm not going with her.'

'She's only come to say goodbye, love. Your own mother.'

'How do you know?' Penny flushed and stuck out her lip. Bertha Cope had no idea what to do, and Penny repeated with attack, 'How do you know?' Then she dropped her case and ran, across the yard, round the house, to the old milking sheds, too fast for Bertha to catch up. With a laughing sigh of disregard, Bertha straightened her apron before rushing to tell the others. It was Vera who came with Bertha across to the sheds, bundling old Bertha along. The ground was slushy inside the yards. They took two steps and sank into squelching, impassable mud.

Slackening her determination, Vera stopped and called in a high, singsong voice, 'Pen-ny! Pen-ny!'

There was silence. She said tartly, 'We'd find her in time but we haven't got all day.' And suddenly she didn't care. In the light of the child's disappearing act – the child who thought to run away forever – Vera's leap of illusion fell flat on its face. Penny refused to see her; so with a kind of relief Vera turned back towards the house, told the others to drink up their tea, and rustled them out to the car.

They were quickly gone. Penny's back was pressed against the single fat gum tree on the hill of the home paddock: the horizon, as far as anyone looking from the house was concerned. She was flat against the bark, her arms squeezed to her sides, her heart beating like a drum. She feared her panting might give her away. But only the sheep knew she was there.

Not until she felt well and truly safe did she come out of hiding, and not for many years afterwards did she see her mother again. When Penny went up to Adelaide for school, meetings were arranged. By then Penny was on the offensive. Whenever they met she forced Vera to laugh about the little girl who had charged through mud and pressed her back against the only tree in a wide open paddock.

# 4 • THE ROAD, 1946-1950

JACK TREGENZA WAS A YOUNG MAN then. Twenty-five. A youth in most people's language. In Jack's case, though, no one doubted his maturity. Like all the boys who had been to war, Jack had seen more than he ought. Of the two brothers, only Jack had returned alive, the elder brother at that. Young Peter was the mother's favourite. Jack came back from the war with the burden of making amends.

Not that Irene Tregenza was oversensitive. She was as tough as her best old cow's worn-out udder. Not a word of recrimination was ever said against Jack. Only once, when the telegram came with news of Jack's return, did Irene cry, with despair not joy, sobbing Peter's name, because she wanted the good news to be of him. Vera saw, and the postmistress, no one else. But people assumed, as their way of explaining Jack's seriousness, that Irene had never forgiven him.

Jack grew into a man who made sacrifices naturally, as if he deserved no better, or hadn't the guts to fly in the face of his responsibilities. Breaking with family tradition, he took a job that required a clean shirt every day, in the stock and station agency. He worked in his shirt sleeves and was sound with the paperwork. The rest of his time he spent at the shack by the beach, a home more spartan than the barracks and more solitary than a monastery. That's what he liked. His mother's dairy farm was just across the paddocks down a straight bit of rough road;

he called in there each day; she cooked and washed for him; but he was separate.

Irene had enough on her hands, anyway, with Vera's baby. Motherhood wasn't easy to take on at her age, when even her cows were getting to be too much. But there was nowhere else for Penny to go. Irene sang and prattled to the kid as she got the cows milked, lugged cans about in her great boots, hosed down stalls smelling richly of cud, steam, chaff, and wood wet with piss. Penny toddled in the hoof-stomped mud of the yards as if it were her element. Poor wee poddy-calf, she was Granny's joy. Irene would gasp for breath and rest against the railing, finding herself grinning in a shock of happiness – Penny two-years-old, running ahead of her across the yard to the house. To think that the child was all that remained of her son Peter was a second order of mystery. She hadn't taken Penny on in any such high-minded spirit. She was simply landed with her. The curse of her old age, she joked to Jack. But she never let the strain penetrate her broken-toothed smile.

When Jack entered the house, he would pick Penny up and hold her in his arms, slobbering big rubbery lips against her and making her eyes pop in a mixture of apprehension and adoration. They talked closely from the time before Penny could form words. Even at three years old when she hated to be picked up, Jack still did so and Penny let him. He asked how she was and told her things that were new and funny. 'Penny wise, pound foolish!' he would always reply when she produced a saying. He put on an act to keep her entertained, the one thing that could improve his own humour. Sometimes he and Penny were kids together under his old mother's stern eye. Other times he joined Irene's anxious adult speculations about Penny's future.

'When are you two girls going to give away the cows and come and live with me?' Jack would pretend to grumble.

'What would become of this little one then?' Irene would interject. 'The milk business is doing very nicely thank you, sir.'

The skin was loose around the old woman's neck and pulled tight when she swallowed, making breathing painful. Despite her tiredness, her faith was unshakeable. As long as Penny needed her, her strength would keep coming, till she wore herself to nothing. She prayed only that she would last.

What Jack contemplated, alone in his shack, was a different matter. Unlike the young husbands of his age, unlike other young men who keenly anticipate the lusts of the next twenty-four hours or next seven days, Jack left alone what lay ahead. What might be was like the ocean at its most serene, or the night at its most muffling, not crisscrossed by his fretting or coloured by his dreams. He was ready for whatever might come, as he lay on his bed, the sheet across his bare chest, his hands tucked behind his head, his vacant eyes to the ceiling. He had no fear of the night noises, or of his own nightmares. Perhaps his imagination had worn out in the Borneo jungle, where he lost even the capacity to distinguish sweet hibiscus from green human flesh, and by chance survived, a fact that meant nothing more than that. Yet the past was clear to him. He knew who lived and who had died, who had gone and who stayed. Straightforward. Not to be thought about. He had been lucky.

Lying on his bed, he thought of his mother and the child across the paddock in their solid house. At the edge of the shore in his tin-roofed shack, on top of the low cliff, Jack was their protector. Whether he lay awake at night or slept, he was keeping vigil. That was the place he'd found. If the moths came whirling crazily round the lamp or the mozzies buzzed like devils in his ears, he knew to switch off the light and the moths would go, or light the green coil to drive the insects away. Likewise, he would simply shoulder and bear the other things to come.

On one such unperturbed summer's night the knocking came, like a bit of wind, at the shack door. Uncovered on his bed, Jack stirred from sleep without knowing why. It was the coldest hour of the night, towards dawn, and there was not the light to which he usually woke. He hovered there between sleep and wakefulness, pleasurably, as if his stiff mattress had levitated like a magic carpet. The knocking came again, a hollow rat-a-tat which he denied at first, though the noise wasn't customary. When the knocking came for the third time, he was fully alert and almost jumped to his feet. Putting on his old dressing-gown he went to the back window and gave a wide survey of the shadowy, dawn-silver land, frozen in quietude. Then a movement close in caught his eye. He opened the door and found Penny there behind the wire screen. Quickly he brought her inside and knelt by her, holding her in his arms while he asked what had happened. She wore pink-striped pyjamas and the rubber boots she used for going about the cowyard. Her hair was mussed from sleep and her ruddy skin was cold. She had walked by herself all the way from the farm to Jack's shack.

She had heard a noise and woken in the night and called to Granny Irene, called and called without getting an answer. At last she had switched on the bedside light and gone timorously down the hall to Irene's bedroom. From the doorway she saw her lying there, motionless and staring, and called to her again, this time in a whisper. With each unanswered whisper she crept a step forward, each step dispelling her fear as knowledge and courage took over. When she reached the bed and saw the old face that would not answer, that held its position now, fixed and empty, the shell of a spirit, she put out her hand and touched Granny Irene's cheek. There was no response, nothing. Penny withdrew her hand in horror, and thought. Then, more seriously, she laid her hand on Granny Irene's forehead and said goodbye.

At four years old Penny understood that she was the only living one in Granny Irene's house and that she had to take the news to Jack. She sat down in the chair, curled in a ball, and watched. She hoped that Granny Irene might suddenly sit up again, jump out and ask what on earth was up. She wondered if something would come to take Granny Irene away: she tried to keep her eyes open in case. She didn't want to leave, and in the end she couldn't help falling asleep. When she woke up, Granny Irene was lying there as if a hundred years had passed. Behind the curtains was a dim glow of light. Penny got out of the chair without looking too closely at the dead body, and went to put on her boots as if Granny Irene had called her out early to help with the cows. She opened the back door and went out alone into the yard, following the path to the drive, though the world was not visible. She walked down between the black pines, familiar and changed, and turned with small determined child's steps on to the road. The air was chilly. She had no fear. This land was her friend. Even in her present numbness her heart recognized each landmark of the way, until the sea was in sight, a stranger colder matter in the grey suspension before dawn. She watched where she was going, walked without stopping, until she reached the door of Jack's place.

'Granny Irene's dead,' she said. 'Granny Irene's dead. She's lying in her bed and stopped breathing.'

She buried her face against the hot, dark fur of Jack's robe. He wrapped her in his arms, stroked her, wordless himself, until he said, 'We better go.'

Jack's first thought was to quell the terror that had made Penny come to him in the night. To doubt what she said was secondary. In the car his own fear rose; he felt bloodless and sick. If something had happened but not death, every second would count. Or already it would be too late. They disrupted the peaceful order of the house when they burst in, but once they reached the half-dark bedroom they saw there was no need to rush or panic. Irene was laid out with an unfussy dignity such as her spirit would have approved. Staring at the fact, Jack silently thanked God – thanked his mother – that the end was so straightforward. She had, as was her strength, spared them suffering, gone in the middle of things as she would have wanted. Jack was not unprepared for the shock. He closed her eyes, straightened the sheet, and put his arm around Penny, who stood beside him.

'She kept us all going,' he said. 'Now we'll have to manage by ourselves, won't we? I suppose the first thing to do is have some breakfast. Then we'll go into town and see about the arrangements. You've had a long night, eh?'

In the kitchen Jack made a hearty breakfast for the two of them. Moving among his mother's things, his mother's order, he was invested with her presence. They ate hungrily at her table as the sun rose with white-gold shafts through smoky trees and cast a hot square on the kitchen floor. The morning lowing of cattle, pained basso groaning, might have been grief.

Jack said, 'We mustn't forget the cows tonight.'

Head bowed over her plate, Penny began to cry.

After the service she stood outside the church in the sun, and held Kath Hocking's hand. With the pallbearers Jack was getting the flower-strewn box into the back of a hearse. Caught by the light, the wood was reddish. The handles shone. Auntie Kath's palm was sticky as she sniffed, dabbing her nose with a crushed hankie.

She said, 'They don't come like that any more. What a trot she's had.'

Eight miles to go down a straight white road to the cemetery. Jack rode in front beside the undertaker. Penny went in the back seat of the Hockings' car. Kath thought it wrong for a child to see the coffin dropped down into the mushroom-coloured peninsula earth, but Jack insisted. The child had understood more than that already.

Penny stood in the straight line between Jack and Kath Hocking. Kath's husband Les was on the right. The ground was dry and sandy, clumped together with burnt-off grass. The damp pile of dug-up earth steamed as it dried in the blazing sun. For the rest, the graveyard consisted of neat plots, bright marbles, faded artificial flowers and patches of yellow buffalo grass where the council had watered – a small stake reclaimed for the time being from rolling indeterminate scrub and sand. The minister said his words without rhetoric, and it was quickly finished.

As they crossed to the car, Les Hocking made a speech: 'We think of you as part of the family, Jack. Kath and I want you to know that. We're here whenever you need us. That goes for Penny too. The lass gets on well with our kids. One more mouth to feed is no problem. We'd be happy to take her in. Think it over. We can offer her a good home.'

Jack bristled. 'I'll be stopping over at the farm now. See to the cows. Penny and me will stick together for the time being. I reckon that's best. Till we sort things out. Thanks for the offer, anyway. Much appreciated.'

In the circumstances, no one minced words.

'It's always there,' said Les. They shook hands again. 'Sincere condolences.'

Kath had tears in her eyes when she kissed Jack. She had put Les up to making the offer. If it was the obvious thing by Kath's all-nurturing lights, it was also a reminder of what Jack had missed: a good home-maker and a good home – what life reduced to in the end. 'We're thinking of *you*, Jack,' she said warmly. And, since they were in their funeral best, she turned and slipped her arm through Les's.

Penny climbed in the back. Her little feet scarcely reached the floor. Jack climbed in after her, protectively. Les said the others who'd gone straight from the church to the pub would've picked over the best of the refreshments at the wake, leaving nothing for those poor souls who had made the trip to the graveyard. While the grown-ups grinned, bucking themselves up, Penny gazed outwards at the pale, low, unpeopled hills flashing by.

\* \* \*

Jack remembered a conversation. Sensed rather than heard, its distant echoes were as sweet as the primrose flowers of mignonette in spring, yet as sour as the crushed stalks of springtime yellow soursobs. Above the Peesey Point jetty, on the headland, he and Kath were walking on a Sunday afternoon at some time of the year, neither winter nor summer, when the world seemed far away. The sea was a silk of pewter purple, with threads pulled where the wind currents ran. The tide was around the blackened steps of the old jetty, which grew out of the water on massive wooden piers. Across the bay to the north-east, at a distance no nearer than the horizon, was another country marked by sand, and as they strolled round the headland to the west they could see with clarity the spit of Point Mirracowie, and the solitary sentinel tree.

'Jack, Les and I are going to get married,' Kath said. Her thick, dark curls were just long enough to catch the breeze and pull away from her brow. Her cheeks were blooming. Her wide hips swayed, brushing against Jack as she walked, her hands clasped with inner contemplation.

She had reached the decision through natural good sense, not ecstasy. As Jack grasped its implications, he offered congratulations and added quizzically, 'I'm sure you'll be very happy.'

Her reply was slightly barbed. 'I can't wait forever.'

'There's no danger of that. At your age.'

'It's good to get these things sorted out,' she said, 'for a woman.'

She had a woman's capacity to wait, but no wish to consecrate herself to a notion, which Jack seemed tacitly to be asking of her. She had waited all through the war, keeping his photograph, writing regular, unanswered letters. He was her boy, her natural match. She had never stopped hoping for his return; her hope, she believed, had played its part. They had known each other all their lives. In the same class at school neither was flashy or unusually talented, both being the middling sort who were expected to triumph only in decency, reliability, kindness and the carrying-on of things while other people tried to change the world. Dull they were not, but friendly and endearing. When Jack went off to war, nineteen and bound for the Middle East with the 2/3rd Machinegunners of the 7th Division, he put his fears into simple words for Kath. He merely wished that he would keep his head when things got baffling. She kissed him on the steps of the jetty while music from the farewell dance still rang in their ears, and the moonlight on the water and their tender cuddling made it easy to say that the world was worth fighting for.

Today they passed the same place, the jetty steps. But now they passed almost as unconnected people. They kept walking, back around the cove to the shack where baby brother Peter, and Vera and Val and Jack and someone else too – young Vera's date of the time, someone else gone – had got giggly on rum and coke (of all things) and made so much whoopee that they laughed till they cried and toppled down the steps on to the sand on Jack's last night home: January 1940.

'You couldn't do much better than Les,' said Jack. 'Well, I don't have to tell *you* that. He's good with people. He'll get that place paid off in no time. He won't sit still then either. He's a good bloke, Les. You can trust him. He'll be in demand for that.'

'I told Les it was just kid stuff between you and me. He's got a lot of time for you, Jack. You need drawing out, he says.'

'I've been drawn out once too often,' laughed Jack. 'Wanna go down?'

There was a steep path to a horse-shoe shingle-covered cove where Peter and Jack used to skim stones. Sometimes they would row there from the shack, in the little dinghy. In the war a supply of arms was kept in a cave under the clifftop there, in case the Japanese subs got round the bottom of the continent. The locals were ready to attack.

Jack gave Kath his hand to help her down the sheer track. Loose stones cascaded in front of them as they slipped.

He had been drawn out alright – by Vera Binns, who called herself Vera Tregenza at the time he was thinking of, with a ring on her finger she reckoned Peter had given her at the Registrar of Births, Deaths and Marriages in Adelaide. She and the baby had still been living in Granny Irene's house on the farm, shaping their life to Peter's return in spite of what they knew. Peter's return was a fiction, fading daily, loosening itself from their grip, but Jack found it unbearable even to be near such futile hope. He needed something ordinary and actual to make up for the war, and the baby was that. Vera resented him, derided his experience as a P.O.W., called him a lump. She said it was a mistake that he'd come home in Peter's place. She told him to go back and turn himself in. He didn't mind her saying it. One of the lucky ones, moping round the yard helping Vera hang up nappies only six months since his discharge, he felt that way himself.

When Kath came to visit, Vera was always sweet as pie to Jack. Standing with Kath out the back, Vera would admire Jack's clumsy way with an axe. For afternoon tea she would bake the biscuits Jack liked. Gladly she would give Kath the baby to nurse, so she could recline like a Victory girl. Or, if they were out walking, she would link arms with Jack and stride ahead with the wind in her hair.

Poor Kath was placid and doleful at Jack's lack of response to her. They still went out together on Saturday nights. She assumed that they would marry, and talked to him unassertively of her hopes. But since the war he was different, as if he had no life of his own. She wanted to understand, but he wouldn't talk about it. He was content to let her plan and prattle, but remained cheerfully indifferent, unable to share. He sometimes responded to her suggestions with a weird, unseeing stare and rigidly clamped hands. Then he'd grin. He refused to divulge what was in his mind – a stubbornness which Kath couldn't budge. Once, Jack had sobbed on her breast, with fists pounding against her neck like a snivelling baby. Kath would have preferred it if he had put the hard word on her – not that she would've given in.

One day Vera came to see Kath at home, a particular and rare occasion for the women to be alone together. Vera was wearing a fashionable, home-made yellow dress and a matching buttercup hat, and frothed with chatter. She'd left the baby with Irene and might have been any young lass out and about on a Saturday afternoon: her flushing colour and darting eyes were far from maternal. Kath's two little brothers stopped and writhed, paying court to her, as they passed through the lace-curtained parlour. In the kitchen Kath's mum listened to the wireless; its crackle drowned the whispers of the two pert girls out front on the settee.

'Jack's such a sweetie,' began Vera, showing a kneecap as she crossed her legs. 'He positively dotes. Most men wouldn't bother with a little bubba. They'd be put off. I can hardly tear him away to get a word in myself.'

Kath smiled at Vera's frivolous astonishment. She knew Jack's tenderness. 'I suppose the little one reminds him of Peter,' was her reply. 'Sorry, does it hurt you to talk about him?'

Vera lowered her eyelids to the floor. 'It stabs me every time I hear his name. I try not to think – ' she shuddered, ' – poor darling. It's too horrible. That's the funny thing about Jack . . .' She looked squarely at Kath. 'He's the spitting image of his brother in so many ways. Not to look at, I don't mean. He's not a looker like Spinner. But his little ways are the same. I can never see Jack with the baby without I think it's Spinner there. It gives me a real warm feeling, not the sick taste I get when I think of him other times. When Jack's holding that bubba, in the shadow – you know – when I can't see his hair and that,

I could swear he was the father come back. Nothing funny, nothing like that, Kath. It's just that brothers are very close.'

'Too close, aren't they, in the church's eyes?'

Nothing had changed in Kath's appearance, but the anger in her neck and spine was a rod of iron.

'What's the church got to do with it?' Vera spoke breathily, holding back her giggles. 'Oh that!' She slapped Kath. 'You naughty thing, you do jump ahead. You mean if I'm already married to Peter?'

'Aren't you?'

Affectedly, taking her time, Vera adjusted her position on the settee. 'Anyway, let's not talk about Jack any more. Men are a pain.'

Her point made, she changed the subject to dressmaking. In her airy manner she had communicated her assumption that Kath had no claim on Jack. Almost enlisting Kath's aid, she had offered her daring plan – to marry Jack, to get her child a father and herself a Mr Tregenza – in such a way that Kath could not protest. Her rival listened with a polite smile, a regrettable acquiescence that began to make real what Vera intimated. Kath was hurt, but wouldn't show it. She felt plain and vulnerable against brazen Vera. If there was something already between Vera and Jack – and Lord knows Jack would need some pretty fancy footwork to keep out of her clutches – it would explain why he had slipped away from his warm bond with Kath into that limbo of detachment and sad, nervous self-apology. Vera had come to tell Kath to give Jack up, and Kath was noble enough to comply, if compliance was asked of her, in the interest of the greater good – if Vera could bring Jack back to life. But Kath wouldn't take Vera's word for it. First she must tackle Jack directly, even if it meant making a fool of herself.

We get used to reality, thinking we know the resistant woodgrain we have been working for years. How does the reliable shape we have seasoned turn in an instant to illusion? Or if not an instant, in Val's case, then a long afternoon's re-assessment following some remarks dropped like stray seed. Soon the new plant germinates and grows into all the reality there is. By evening, when practical, self-doubting Kath was ready to confront Jack, the long wait for union with him was already over.

Normally they would have gone to the pictures in the local hall.

'I don't feel like it tonight,' she said. 'Do you mind? I hope you weren't counting on it. I'd like to have a little talk instead.'

He had the car, and they stopped in darkness out along one of the roads.

'I want things clear between us,' she said. 'Are we engaged?'

'No – ' his inflection rose, 'not officially.'

'Is it going to stay that way?' she asked.

'That's just how it's been.' He was more evasive than he needed to be. He resisted the future, hated to juggle with it. He didn't know why Kath was interrogating him; but perhaps he too, in his silence, in his fancy, thought of Vera, who made offers where Kath made demands.

'Kath – ' he turned again more softly, 'are you counting on me?'

'I can't,' she said, losing her voice.

He assumed she had been working up her courage to that point; he didn't think further. A clumsy stiff arm round her shoulder. No words.

'Well,' he sighed finally, 'better be turning round.'

He crashed the car through a semicircle on the narrow road and they jolted back where they had come.

After that, Jack fell readily into Vera's net. Innocently, as though in a dream, he would push Penny along in the pram on Saturday mornings when Vera was in Wooka shopping. He blushed when Kath hailed them. He chauffeured Vera about, did her business; it could only be a matter of time before the partnership was consummated.

In a spirit of duty, for the sake of his dead brother and the baby, Jack put himself at Vera's disposal, and welcoming his nearness, Vera suffered the restrictions that form imposed on their relationship. With all her wiles, all her craving for love, she led him a dance on clifftop walks or bright beach days, on still domestic evenings by a dying fire, on weekend afternoons in the shack that for both of them shimmered with memories. She was beautiful for him, and he succumbed with a laugh of blind, absent intoxication.

In a pleasant, uninvolved way things brewed between them for weeks, until late one night, after the pub, they were walking down the lane by the corrugated iron fence of the council lot. Vera was stumbling tipsily ahead, laughing with a guttural burr as she threw her head back to the balmy night in an antic gesture of blissful abandon. She halted suddenly and Jack bumbled into her. As their hands fumbled for balance, she turned quickly to be in his arms. They felt each other's hot breath. There was an instinctive, sloppy kiss that went on and on, and she clasped him even as he pulled away.

'We need this, Jack. Forgive me, but it's right. Believe me. We both need this.'

He disengaged himself roughly, clumsily, and staggered forward a few steps. Then he stopped in his tracks and stared horrified at an image that Vera had construed so differently. He saw her plan – his idiocy – and unable to face her he blurted, 'I can never be that to you. You're Peter's.'

Vera's whole form was marble white in the night light. 'You can't be his brother,' she said. 'Not a miserable specimen like you.'

She started to cry. 'Just forget it, Jack. Forget all about this. For the baby's sake. No one knows how hard it is, so slow and sluggish and desperate. I'm sorry. Just take me home.'

'I didn't realize,' he said.

'You wouldn't.'

But that was the funny part. Although Vera's plan backfired, Jack missed out on Kath too, whose pride was wounded. She blamed him for the dismissal which Vera had engineered and wouldn't give him another chance. Maybe he preferred it that way. He was so slow in those days that he seemed not the full quid, dumb, lacking somehow. Rather than be fought over, he became a thing not worth fighting for.

So, a year later, as they slithered down the gravel to Pebble Cove, although Jack's bulk steadied her, Kath was really leading Jack, like a half-wit, to accept her decision to marry Les Hocking, the decent bloke in the council office whose gammy leg had kept him out of war service and allowed him not to blot his copybook with her during five years of worship from afar.

Kath felt more sorrow than Jack, who seemed not to realize that the news condemned him to perpetual bachelorhood. Now that Vera had gone up in smoke, Kath considered Jack had no prospects other than the proferred hand of friendship.

'You deserve it, Kath,' he said. 'You must feel full of prospects. You set your sights, and when things come in reach, you take them. It reminds me of when we were kids, watching the nautilus come in, frantic on the beach because we couldn't make them come any faster. They came in the end.'

'Don't make it sound small,' she chuckled. 'My hands are going to be full as full. Lord give us strength!'

Under their feet the shingle clinked like grinding cogs, grey and pink and white. Across the water on its biscuit promontory, Jack's tree seemed very near, as delusively near as the stick in a game of quoits.

It was the beatification of Peter that Vera couldn't stand, though she was wrong to blame Jack. He accepted himself as the lesser brother and never made a song and dance over Peter's memory. Irene was the one who wouldn't let them forget, as her way of testing and chiding Vera, of whom, for reasons of blood and history, she had never approved.

A raggle-taggle set of itinerants, the Binnses had moved up and down the west coast as shearers, barmaids, day labourers and household help, keeping the Wooka district bereft of a settled family to observe, evaluate and respect. They were people who never stuck at things, doing neither harm nor good. They had no place of their own – out of choice, Irene assumed. (Irene was a great blamer.) The dear old boy and girl who were Vera's parents had done wonders, of course: their daughter was so pretty and modern you would not believe she came from such broken stock. From an early age Vera had felt the appraising sharpness of Irene Tregenza's kind. From suffering an inferiority for which she was not responsible, Vera had developed a supersubtle sense of where she fell short, and how to remedy it within the limits of her girlish power. Her study of other people – their clothes, speech, and regard or disregard for fellow human beings – yielded a pointed political understanding of the stony rural community where she lived. Property, birth, money, graciousness, subservience, know-how, and positions won by perseverance – she understood the laws. What an incalculable joy when she was singled out by the eyes of Peter Tregenza, the darling younger son for whom everything was reserved. (Rightly so, because stolid Jack had nothing of Peter's flair. In any case Jack was away at the war and would never come back.)

There is a photograph of Peter in his cricket whites – a pretty youth with bleached hair cropped close round his rather large ears; tanned skin; and expressionless eyes accustomed to survey land and sea before narrowing in on a target. The photograph does not show his self-seeking quality, however, nor that his young eyes were green and sensual, dully waiting to be enlivened by pleasure and triumph. Though of middling height and finely built, Peter had a sportsman's developed chest and shoulders. His walk had the merest swagger, with an economy of movement that belonged to the dancing athlete inside the gangling farmboy. He was only fifteen when he first played cricket for the district. He was a charmed spin bowler and loped towards the pitch with his face screwed, squinting in a fiendish grin. They nicknamed him Spinner. The men said he played batsmen with the same technique his old dad, Willie, had used for fish. He had a sleepy red mouth, high cheeks still chubby, and a sly, spare way of speaking: long silences broken with long ripe expletives. All those attributes made Spinner Tregenza the star of the peninsula's younger set. Nor could the elders help making a potential hero of the lad, though some wagged their fingers and refused to be dazzled by the promise of youth.

Hope was an easy compensation for the generation of Irene Tregenza, who had known hard times and fraying despair. Irene had married late because she was, as some said, so capable or so untender that she frightened men off. At a marriageable age she was already the force behind her parents' dairy business, so couldn't leave their home. Instead she stayed put and accepted a man who was a fisherman. She continued to manage the farm which her husband used as a refuge when he came on shore. He wasn't a settler. As soon as he sold a catch he was gone again for weeks. When conditions were wrong and he stayed at home with his wife, the surf tunnelled through the living room. Willie had taken a wife because he had no one else. He was older than Irene, having squalled into the world the day Ned Kelly was hanged in 1880. Such is life.

Willie Tregenza was a gentle, modest man, with a sparkling eye and a vast capacity for undertakings. Once he found her, he knew a good woman in Irene. And if she couldn't quite contain her good man, her estimation of him was diminished not one jot. Willie loved the two boys, born – some years apart – when he was too old to expect such arrivals. He'd sired another kid years ago, when he was a pup working on the railway at Wangaratta, off a Chinese girl. The suffering mother. Almost outside memory, his shame. He'd never stayed. Now these two boys were like a forgiveness, fabled little sea-beasts tossed up by unheard-of waves. Defying their mother, he loved to take them out in the boat, to teach them to hold the rope and feel the line. Scamps! Scallywags! How Willie howled and scowled at them, and little Peter always howled back, laughing as though nothing and no one would ever harm him. But Jack preferred the steady land days to the days when his grizzled father tumbled them out to sea.

The Depression days – when special provision was impossible, when survival not growth was the aim – were bad times to have growing children but together the family got through in shipshape fashion. They had milk and butter and fish, which they were also able to hand on to others.

Jack was a solemn manly chap in secondary school, and Peter the flower of promise, when Willie Tregenza failed to return from one of his regular fishing trips. His disappearance was never explained, and Irene showed no interest in the various conjectures. She accepted her neighbours' charity and the insurance money with equal practicality. Unlike the farm and the cows, her beloved Willie had never been a permanent feature of the landscape. She smiled fondly for him whenever she saw a billowing cloud or a craft scudding at full tilt across the blue. His boat was washed up on a beach south of Point Light, dropped on the sand without damage, like one of the kids' toys. There was no telling how many leagues she had drifted homewards, in good enough nick for another fishing boat to tow her round to harbour at Mirracowie Bay. The boat was heaved up the ramp into the boatshed and the doors were locked until one of Willie's sons would be old enough to put out in her again.

After the loss of her husband, Irene's reason was Peter, not Jack. Peter would take over the farm and transform it, buying up neighbouring properties, coordinating the other producers, pooling the district's dairy production into one large plant for manufacture and distribution. Going automatic. He would get educated in the city and play cricket for Australia. Irene dreamed – unlikely dreams when you looked at charming Peter with his reluctant, enchanting smile. He had too many abilities and a mind for tricks. He was happy with himself and with his gift of making himself feel good.

That side of him, Vera knew, had been open to temptation. She said so to Irene.

Irene made a cult of Peter's memory. His photograph had pride of place on the mantelpiece. His things were carefully, superstitiously stored in drawers. The tiny Saint Christopher, all of him that came back from the war, was kept with Irene and Willie's wedding portrait and the boys' birth certificates in a dog-eared relic of an album that only Irene could touch. Late one evening Vera caught a glimpse of Irene sitting under the standard lamp with the medallion between her fingers catching the light like a miniature halo. Irene stared with shut eyes, trying to experience what Peter must have lived through, what he might have become if only he stood as manfully on the hearth as he stared bravely from his airman's cap on the mantelpiece. Irene refused to see in the photograph something that Vera saw – the beginnings of a pout to Peter's mouth, an almost-stirring of the full flesh she had loved. As far as Irene was concerned the world would go to the dogs because Peter wasn't around to fix it. He was her hero, but it was too late to care now. She had come to content herself with the perfect thing her dead boy might have been. Death worship, which Vera couldn't stand. If Peter had lived, he and Vera would have spat in the old lady's face, would have kicked up their heels and gone spinning out of the wretched district if old Mum didn't let them have their fun – their deserts. Peter could be precious about himself; his saving grace was his hot hunger for a good time. He luxuriated in others' adulation, a golden chap basking in his own radiance, his blood coursing with thin ideals, vain, physical, sweet. Ho! scoffed Vera. A mother's saint indeed!

How the two women grated in the household. Even the baby was a bone of contention, even affable Jack on his daily visits. But Vera had no choice. Revulsion at poverty, and a single mother's good sense, kept her caged.

At the best of times the district was suspicious of strangers. In the years after the war, drawing in on themselves, the local people were more suspicious than ever. One day a solitary, dirty, foreign fellow was reported setting up camp at the base of the Peesey Point jetty. His tent was seen – an ex-army khaki job – and his car was heard clattering down the track. He was sometimes seen fishing, or swimming naked, or walking past in the dust with a dark stare, but mostly he was inside the tent. In the evenings there was a smell of fish cooking on his fire and the sight of his lonely figure moving about behind the smoke and flames. People made a point of walking that way to get a good look. A couple of the men went and tried to start up conversation. The bloke spoke very little English. Weeks of black growth covered his face. Only his high, greasy-skinned nose showed, and his knife-like eyes. Someone said he lived like an animal, but this was disproved when his supplies ran out and he was forced into Wooka to buy soap and toothpaste, along with eggs, bread, beans, butter and a sack of spuds. He had money from somewhere. Afterwards he walked across to the empty pub and, in the mid-morning, drank schooners of beer until his eyes went pink and contented. The publican took the opportunity to ask questions and deduced from the monosyllables of self-taught English that he was a Yugoslav sailor, a single refugee who had made his own escape before the end of the war, with no help from the organization, waiting no man's counsel, who had fled from the spectre of communism to the end of the earth: Australia. His name was Stanislav Petchek. As a sailor he had the means. The only honourable living he could make in the new land was as a fisherman. So he was travelling now, living in his tent, in search of a place to start. He was strong and skilled. When the publican suggested that one of the local fishing families might take him on, he pounded the bar to say he would always be his own boss. That was the end of question time.

Word passed around, and when Jack Tregenza heard of the bloke camping down by the jetty, he kept a lookout for him. When Stan passed the agency window one day, Jack saw what a bull of a man he was, and called out to him. The man came inside and stood meekly at the counter with hands cupped. Jack couldn't have budged him, but the man listened with respect as Jack related his father's story. Neither of his father's sons was able to carry on the fishing business, Jack explained, so the equipment was up for sale, including the boat. It wasn't new. It had been stored away for years while history intervened. The foreigner would be doing Jack a favour to take it off his hands. They could talk about the terms . . .

Stan neither nodded nor shook his head. Politely he thanked Jack and, confident of his own judgement, communicated his wish to see the boat. An arrangement was made for him to call at the farm that Sunday. As he left, he bowed slightly.

When he came, it was Vera who answered the door, with the baby on her hip and her hair loose from the baby's playing. As she brushed her hair back, her breasts rose beneath her tight jumper. The man's face was black behind the wire. There was nothing clean about him, but as he came in, pausing for her to cross the room ahead of him, he conveyed such mannerly chivalry that she went demurely to fetch Jack instead of yelling.

Jack could sense the man's eagerness. Together they drove to the boatshed and heaved at its stiff doors on their rusted hinges. Jack was ashamed at how long it was since those doors had last opened to receive the light. He felt that he was entering his father's tomb. For years nothing had stirred in that shed, hot and dry and dark with the clean smell of dried weed and fish. Stan put on a brother's piety and moved forward ahead of Jack, laying his searching hands on the boat in reverent love. He grunted, murmured incomprehensibly, whistled through his teeth. He rocked the boat with his great strength, tenderly, testingly. He squeezed and fingered everything. The boat had been expertly laid up. Jack remembered the day. He seemed weirdly to remember the physical action of placing each object there in the shed – the oars, the rowlocks, the bailer, the buoy, the wicker crayfish basket hanging from a hook – all with absolute finality. Stan prowled a bit, giving no sign of a decision, until he indicated that he was ready to go. They drove in silence to the farm where, in a spirit of ritual, Jack offered tea. Stan smiled graciously when Vera brought pikelets, spongecake and the tea things to the little table between the two men in the living room. When she settled with her cup, an auburn-haired goddess of good luck for the transaction, Stan broke his silence:

'I can pay good price.'

The sum named pulled the rug out from under Jack's charity.

'You think she's worth that much?'

'A fine boat. Ready for the sea no time. You want cash?'

Jack was startled. Obviously the man lived his life of deprivation with determined frugality. The generosity Jack had been prepared to show seemed suddenly soft-headed, but anyway he said,

'You needn't pay the whole lot now. At that price I

couldn't be happier.'

Vera spluttered into her tea.

Stan stood and gripped Jack's hand with passion. 'I thank you, my friend.'

Stan was courteous to Vera because he assumed her to be Jack's wife. Later, as he came to understand their stories, his chivalry sharpened. By summer the boat was seaworthy and Stan was out learning the habits of the bay and its fish. The old hands were sparing with their advice but came to his aid when he went wrong. He stayed on in his tent by the jetty, sold his fish, and was happy as a bird, whistling as he fried up his meal on the open fire. Each Sunday morning he stood for thirty minutes at the end of the jetty in an attitude of prayer. He was thankful, and flashed his stumpy great teeth to say so.

That summer baby Penny took her first steps. Vera would take her down to Jack's shack where she played on the sand and dared the mysterious water. Penny was weaned now. Breastfeeding was over. She stumbled along the beach on wobbly, independent legs while Vera lay in the sun like a covergirl, indolent and restless, smoothing her legs. She had recovered her figure. With her face in the sand, she lay kicking her legs in the air, hoping to catch someone's eye, dreaming of the day when her twenty-first birthday would come.

For Stan and Vera, talk was a luxury since both were deprived. When they met on the beach they were excited to talk together, and Vera was patient with Stan's halting English. She had no particular story of her own to tell, but she talked along with Stan's tall tales, joining in as if his adventures were the outward expression of what she had experienced inwardly: poverty, desire, oppression, flight. When the war broke out Stan had found himself in a port city on the Dalmatian coast, in a backwater where the crosscurrents of too many conflicts produced a kind of stagnancy; the area was helpless against the Germans, the communists were waiting coolly in the wings. The people, like tribes, slogged it out against each other. For a while Stan made night crossings to the Adriatic coast of Italy, with guns or men under his tarpaulin, this way or that. He made his money, but it was no war. An inhabitant of a limbo – and more and more at risk – he sensed in the air that he might find himself paralysed in that port city and never move again. Ah, all his father's stories of the '15-'18 war! Caporetto! The heroic exploits! What he lusted after was a war with colour and victory and the glory of revenge, but what he sniffed was a slow ice-age coming for his portion of the world. So he put to sea.

As he talked, twisting, wriggling, giggling on the sand, she knew in herself his fears and lusts. He scarcely disguided his want of her and she responded with a rich, pent-up talent that needed only his audience. She was Rita Hayworth. At first she thought he was an awfully hairy, dirty, foreign beast whose smell was as thick as his accent. She found his hedge of a moustache absurd, as were his ridged nose and doggy eyes. Then she found him beautiful, irresistible, essential, and started to be afraid. He never put a foot wrong. In the street, in front of Jack, he was well behaved to a fault, waiting, watching her take the bait even as he let her run. She played him too, with bouts of frosty restraint that were all her power. They had already, quickly, come to rely on each other when one afternoon Vera was at the beach alone, the child being with Irene, and Stan took up a different posture. He planted himself on the sand beside Vera's towel.

'You walk with me?' he asked.

Knowing it was a commandment, she parried, 'I couldn't do a thing like that, Mr Petchek. What if someone saw us?'

'Maybe.'

His words didn't add up. He stayed there, grinning, playfully kicking her leg that trembled as she held it in the air.

'You're a naughty boy, Stan,' she said, rising casually to

go with him. Somehow his moustache brushed her in that movement, rasped her, nearly tore.

They clambered on rocks to a tongue of sand, inaccessible between Jack's beach and the boulders of Pebble Cove. He helped her down, to lie on the warm white stretch.

'Do you love me, Stan?'

He scooped at her breasts and sucked the brown hard nipples. He made her cry. She felt as if she was riding a wave, or an animal in the wave, from so far and deep did his passion come. As when she had given birth, she could only rejoice in the desire released. She was dazed afterwards, drunk and shocked at herself; and she felt impelled to repeat their encounter, to meet again often, no matter how comically difficult.

Stan asked Vera to marry him. The question was easy.

'You will have my children too?'

'Yes,' she chuckled from her throat, biting his neck, 'yes.'

The same day she gushed the news heedlessly to Irene, who responded with that voice of iron.

'You will not marry that foreign gentleman while you are the mother of my grandchild. You will do your duty. You will not see or mention him again. If you behave yourself, from now on, we may forget what everyone knows already.'

Vera made a strange choking noise and ran to the bedroom where the door slammed. Irene tended to Penny that evening. In the morning Vera was calm and civil. She sat on the grass under a tree in the garden and fed the baby lovingly, playing with the little girl all morning until the time came for her sleep. Her eyes were glazed when they caught Irene's; she wouldn't let the old woman open her mouth. At a certain point during the afternoon, when Penny was sleeping and Irene was out of the way, Vera walked out on to the road with a suitcase. What bitter storms surged in her then, what terrible just needs. She had no way of distancing her helpless passion, or of understanding, on a level deeper than passion, that she had to live, to throw everything away for the chance of a brand-new start. She reached Stan emotionally exhausted and wretched, and made her demand. The late February dusk was stunned by windless heat. There wasn't much time. She knew Irene would be too proud to come and fetch her. She feared Jack – but thin-blooded Jack would obey his mother, never admitting the elemental drive in Vera's shooting-through. In the darkness Stan hauled the boat on to the trailer, with Vera heaving beside him. They dropped the tent, packed up, and set off at a crawling pace that was all his beat-up car could manage. Stan's honey peach was beside him as his new bride, holding his arm all the way down their long road.

A week later Jack got a letter explaining. The sender had the post office address of a fishing town way over on the far-west coast. She was never coming back. She asked Jack to do his best for the child left behind.

The child lay on her back sleeping peacefully in the late afternoon heat. Across the sheet towards her chin moved a slant of sun that would eventually wake her. Blissful and innocent, she slept in the bed where Peter had slept with the same enviable, adorable unawareness. Only Peter had died for it.

The ageing western sky was dusty cream as the old woman came out of the house, crossed the yard past the pepper trees, shushed the barking dogs aroused to see her so purposeful, and proceeded down the drive. Vera had passed that way, dragging her vanity case and not much else, gone without trace like a gipsy on the road, gone to a cosy arrangement she had fixed up to suit herself. Bad blood. Good riddance. Was it on her, for her, that Peter had wasted himself? Irene needed all her iron character to bear that part of a mother's shame, that she had not driven Vera out earlier. Now she was making amends. She had given Vera a good headstart before picking up the telephone to raise the alarm. She blamed Vera for driving her son beyond his mother's gate into the arms of a war and a death never meant for him, and it was her revenge to take back into her household the one piece of Peter's life that properly remained: the baby girl. Yet cheated by her own justice, Irene felt a terrible and bitter emptiness in her heart as she went to close the gate that Vera in her typical slovenliness had left open. It was not Irene's force but Peter's skill that made the gate to swing so fine and free. And if an iron gate had not felt the effect of time, how short that time must be, little more than a moment of apprehension – and he might come safe home down the road at evening after all, to allay his mother's fears. As Irene closed the gate, her ghostly son bobbed up grinning behind her back. When she turned towards the house, he was there swinging on the gate again. Her face was tough and expressionless. She would not look over her shoulder to find nothing. She would not shed a tear.

# 5 • BISCUIT, JUNE-JULY 1945

ACTIVE SERVICE TURNED OUT TO BE another figure of speech. The routine days in Darwin numbed the boys' ardent expectations. When they were not on training exercises they had only to lounge around the camp, whiling away the hours in talk or taking satisfaction from the strange, charged qualities of the weather. The boys feared frustration, knowing that if they thought too much about their wasted energies, the pity would flare into riot and frenzy. A false sense of readiness was therefore maintained. Mentally and physically they were as fit as fiddles, on alert for the call. At heart, stationed in this weird shimmering outpost of their continent, they were glad when each day passed without its coming. The boys didn't want to go out across the water to the nameless islands, except in boasting. They waited like sentries watching for a thief in the night, and no one, least of all Central Intelligence (that joke), knew what was happening in the northern jungle netherworld of serpents and butterflies. The sea protected them, and the wide tidal flats of Darwin and ghostly mangrove swamps were better than any wall. Wandering down to the beach, staring at the lukewarm, lilac unknown, the boys became enchanted rather than vulnerable. But generally they stuck to terra firma, playing the warrior up and down the sleazy streets of Darwin – a city with a grand purpose for the first time in history.

With nothing else out of the ordinary to occupy him

in those days, Peter Tregenza thought a good deal of Vera. She had made him feel incredibly good and he longed to repeat the episode. His body itched for hers. In compulsive dreams he relived the meeting of their vital spirits, the rush that carried him on for days in repeated echoes of the momentum of orgasm, the memory that made his lips curl. He swore to God it would not be the last time. On the streets of Darwin he looked at women with new confidence. They turned their necks to him but he turned cleanly away, striding with the boys as they laughed like hyenas at a passing woman's magnificent knockers. The boys teased him because he was as toey as a colt, groomed to look like Alan Ladd, though he came from a town on the way to nowhere. They told him that, in actual fact, Alan Ladd was a dwarf less than five foot tall, and Peter would dance backwards from their mockery with untouchable arrogance, a handsome flier under the humid, sleepy sun.

In Darwin the commanders were the nearest thing to an enemy. Despite the bustle, the quiet, lazy town made the war a matter of army discipline versus civilian indolence and related temptations. The smallest dispensation was surrounded with red tape. Once you had permission to take an inch, it was understood that you would take a mile. So Peter and his mates would go out on the town, to the bright lights and packed tables of the Chinese cafe across the road from the ruins of the old Grand Hotel. The place was run by an islander called Lily, a broad, flat-nosed woman with fuzzy hair and enough white blood (Dutch perhaps) to allow her to survive in Darwin. She didn't take sides in the war, though she spurred on the young soldiers who soft-shoed drunkenly from her door at closing time. The boys loved to hear her recite the names: Java, Dili, Sourabaya. She smirked at their youth. They could not disentangle the war from stories in their Boys' Own Annuals, even when they heard above their heads the familiar drone of Aussie engines going out to the islands in steady traffic, and sometimes coming back. Their ears were passively attuned; they pricked up only when a rare Jap plane cut into their sky.

In Lily's cafe Peter saw the man who had escaped from the prison camp on Ambon. By luck and wit, having commandeered a motorboat, he had crossed the sea to Darwin, and now sat eating a hearty meal. The boys had heard a dozen versions of his exploit, and variously coloured accounts of his experiences in the camp. The most horrible of these could be recognized from their own nightmares, and when they admitted to themselves that thousands of their countrymen might be enduring worse while they loafed in anticipation, they were seized by rage and a determination to revenge what their imaginations could not grasp – the fell and random nature of war, crueller than any boys' game. They blew their stack, kicked the table and swore: 'I'll get you bastards.' Each and every man pounding the table and stamping on the floor had a brother to save. Peter thought of Jack, who had been missing for three years. The one who had come back alive was a humble, almost miserable, specimen. For all his escapades he did not sit up straight, but bent to his food like a dog. His bones stuck out like nuts and bolts. He did not inhabit his body. His eyes told nothing. As the talk of revenge swelled around him, he grinned faintly and twitched.

'Go and get them others out,' he ordered, or begged.

Peter turned uncomfortably away, to Lily who was refilling a line of glasses behind the bar.

'Where you from?' she asked the blond boy.

'Due south.'

'The other place.' She wiped the sweat from her brow. 'Should've stayed there. Stinks up here.'

She saw a glint between the buttons of Peter's shirt and inserted her finger. 'What's underneath then?'

'Hey!' Peter giggled. 'Say please.' He unbuttoned the top of his shirt and pulled out the tiny gold medallion on its gold chain. 'Saint Christopher,' he explained. 'Good luck to travellers.'

Lily fingered it, feeling its weight. 'Your sweetheart give it you?' Her nail tickled Peter's chest.

He pulled the chain over his head and laid the medallion in Lily's palm. 'This is the first time I've taken the thing off.'

Even with Vera he kept it round his neck.

'You got a girlfriend?' asked Lily. She bit the medallion to test if the gold was real.

'Hey! None of your business,' he grinned. He thought of the letters he had got from Vera since they parted, full of sweet nothings. The weeks were a lifetime.

'Will you marry her?' Lily cocked her head.

'Wouldn't want to keep a lady waiting.'

'Oh, she'll wait. For sure.'

With a rough, disdainful gesture Lily pushed the medallion into Peter's fist. The charming young man would need protection against the gods. 'Go on, put it away,' she ordered lewdly. 'Don't lose it.'

Later, as the boys were leaving, Lily called Peter over. 'Show me your thing again,' she whispered so the others could hear, again scratching his chest. He couldn't help dissolving in coy giggles. Lily winked over the fair boy's shoulder at the other men, mostly dark-haired and older, who watched and waited in the half-light. 'Better take your cute friend home,' she sighed, pushing Peter's weight away from her bosom and the counter.

In the street, as he adjusted himself, Peter commented, 'I hope I survive this war.'

They laughed raucously.

'I wish I was going out tomorrow.' He couldn't wait to cross the enemy line.

Peter's turn came to move out to the base at Cape Arnhem where a squadron of Mitchells sat in surveillance in case a lone Jap crossed into five hundred miles of unguarded Australian coastline. The place was even quieter than Darwin, nothing more than a tiny huddle of men fenced off from the eroded cliffs and flats of the rainbow country. Down to the water at evening the blacks came, the men with spears and nets, the women with children, and one lovely girl wading up to her belly in the sea. They made slow, easy shadows on the beach at twilight. When they leapt or laughed, breaking the stillness and making a splash, they scarcely disturbed the scene. You couldn't catch the movement with your eye, as when a fish jumps. Other times the same blacks were seen in their ragged clothes stretched in the dust outside shanties in the settlement, their faces a mask of red ugliness and despair. They weren't even voting citizens of the country, Peter thought. Was the war theirs? Was he fighting for them – or against them, in defence of his own people's possession of the land? When these people played in the sea their bright smiles were both innocent and derisive.

Peter hung around the camp when he was not on uneventful reconnaissance flights out over the water. He composed fervent letters to Vera, and sent off a diary record to his mother. There was not much to say. Irene's letters were sad and emphatic about the boy's absence. Vera expressed anger that she couldn't have him in her arms.

The letter from Vera was brought on to Peter at Cape Arnhem after sitting about in Darwin for days. Powder blue and scented, it contained equally perfumed admissions and professions. Vera Binns was in a pickle. She felt no shame; she was exalted, closer to him than ever, no matter if a continent divided them and no one knew what would come. She pleaded with Peter, if he loved her, to back her up. Perhaps a darling wife and child waiting would bring him home more quickly, more safely.

He should have written back at once. But he was reluctant to deceive his mother, who regarded secrecy as gutlessness. Chuffed by his potency, he vowed not to waste his seed in future . . . as he lay itching on the bed.

The following morning there was a special parade after mess. Peter's group was ordered to transfer across the Arafura Sea to the island of Morotai in the Moluccas. No more routine runs. This time they were to fly out and stay there. They had been on indefinite transfer to the coastal surveillance base; now, unexpectedly, they were moving out to the islands. There seemed no plan in what was happening to them – or great changeability and confusion on high.

The squadron leader snorted when Peter asked if there was time to get a letter off.

'This is war, Tregenza!'

They had been ordered to Morotai to stage the dress rehearsal for a battle, the final one, that would finish off the Japanese in the islands, from Timor to the top of the Philippines, and rescue the Australians' sisters and brothers.

The floor of the jungle was not so much mud as a bog of leaves and roots sodden by rain, black as decay. You went up to your knees and knocked your soft bones against the hidden roots, and wasted yourself pulling the leg out for the next step, when to stay would have been easier. Then the shot would come. There was a track they followed, but where they had come from and where they were going meant nothing. To contemplate such abstractions was a futile luxury. All your strength – moral determination when every last pretence of physical strength had gone – was required to push forward only one step at a time through the black corridor of wet jungle. Strange to consider that your last reserves should be used in compliance. Thought, protest, was too painful, too enormous. Their group were the last men left, and perhaps he was the last of them now. He had heard many shots on this march, and less than a hundred men had set out, most of them dying or doomed. There had been more than a thousand originally. At last the steady mathematics of reduction made it his turn, and he might be alone, if he was lost or separated or if the miserable Japanese guards had sunk into the slime themselves. The thought came to him in elemental form that of all the prisoners, all the men, his fellows, there was now only him, looking for the will to take another step. A stick insect, crawling. His eyes ached in their pouches. The clattering of his teeth, a puzzling sensation, the only one he could be sure of. His wasted, feverish body, skin and bone, and bones rotting at that, seemed the strangest habitation for this last dogged fading of his life. The others had been starved, kicked, shot, gripped by disease, fever, despair, had been worked to death. The same things had happened to him; but for some reason he was to be the last to collapse under the burdens imposed. This was not to be imputed to any special quality. Quite random. It didn't ultimately matter. But he was the last and alone. His head was fuzzy and his mind was almost extinguished, and how lovely to sit down and sleep. But because he was convinced of his isolation he became, in the smallest way, free and enterprising. He took a step off the path, the one almost unthinking way he could prove his freedom. The effort and decision were glorious; in the back of his head he waited for the explosion. Beyond the path was a sharp drop into an eerie green webbing of leaves and the black mattress underneath, in a place as unknown and unaiding as the beginnings of life. As he stepped, he slipped, tumbled, rolled into an animal ball and careered. The falling went on; he unbalanced himself so he would drop as far down the mountain as possible. In the green world where he opened his eyes, his cheek against spongy wood and mulch in his mouth, he delicately fingered a wound and his red blood startled him. He turned his head upright and listened. There was water. He slithered further downwards through tunnels of leaves, and splashed into a flowing stream. He drank. He was refreshed. There were snails in the water. He smashed them on a rock and ate the flesh. He knew he must not stay in the water. Its current encouraged him downstream. He came to a clear place. He thought he could rest there. He thought he might find some fish. There were tiny black berries he ate, peppery and acrid. He ate a flower. He thought he must find a hollow where he could be warm and not too wet overnight. It would be his last night on earth. He did not deceive himself. Only he wanted to savour the earth's comforts. But the pain and weakness were too great and he passed out. He was conscious next of dawn rising and his gut wrenching, and black slime trickling uncontrollably from his bowel. Then he dared to moan, believing himself at least to be alone, the last man. A figure in clothes broke through the hanging ferns on the opposite bank and called to him in high jabs. The fellow's skin was like toffee, and his black eyes were frank and sharp. The fellow waded across the stream to Jack, who was shuddering. He touched Jack lightly, then receded. When he was gone, Jack savoured the dream. Then the man returned with another man and a stretcher made of bark on which to carry the pitiful flesh of their find.

So Jack was taken to an encampment and gloomily observed, because he was surely dying, and transferred to a village where he could be inspected by an officer of the Dayak forces operating in that area. Although it was little more than a gesture of good will to pass a dying man over to his comrades, the native guerillas hurried before Jack died to get him to the Australian commandos of Z Force with whom they had been in contact since the capture of Tarakan Island.

That was the first arm of the mopping-up activities in Borneo, the plan orchestrated by MacArthur and rehearsed by the Australians on Morotai. In putting the plan into performance the Australians had lost eight hundred and ninety-two men. Meanwhile the Americans had in the wings the weapon to end all weapons – and the heavy casualties of the final campaigns in the islands would be judged by history a bagatelle of the war, a perfectionist's divertissement that Australia complied with at grievous cost. But in June 1945 there was no thought of judgements to come. The boys were out to free their brothers and win the day. Glory was within their grasp. The convoys flew out from Morotai stacked with bombs which they were eager to drop. Peter's body shook deliriously. Below him the sea was a spread of green-gold scales. Below him was the oil refinery of Balikpapan.

The air strike was massive, fire all round. Suddenly Peter's plane was out of control. The machine dove. Although he rode the plane between his thighs like a beast, he could not make it soar. The machine dropped. As he spiralled helplessly, he had never felt such exhilaration.

When the aircraft crashed, Peter was sliced up. He crawled free before the wreckage exploded and hid in a bombed-out cellar for three days and three nights while the fighting continued. He had his water bottle, nothing else. His front was matted with blood and he didn't dare open his shirt to investigate. When peace fell, a scalped, drawling American patrol found him and took him to hospital.

Huge and cavernous, the Balikpapan hospital, converted from a pompous Dutch administrative building, was chaotic and crowded. In addition to the hundreds of sick and wounded Allied troops, there were also the sick the Japanese had abandoned in their flight. An annexe was erected beside the main entrance where people with minor injuries could be laid out under awnings of woven leaves. On the assumption that his was a surface wound, Peter was placed with the group outside, at the end of the queue for medical attention. He was ruddy in the face still, and enthusiastic about the war despite his throbbing chest. Only days before, he had been lolling and eating up in a camp on Australian soil. In truth, as he lay there watching the comings and goings, he didn't feel too bad. He was light-headed, with no sensation in parts of his body, and his mind was wandering. He considered that a fair few of his bombs had been on target, and was proud to take to himself some responsibility for the operation's success. At other times the stinging in his chest was so great that he closed his eyes and fantasized.

There were native peddlers, forbidden to enter the hospital proper, who came warily at first, then with the confidence of offering a service, among the patients lying outside. A local girl with a basket of fruit hidden under a cloth on her arm came by Peter. What he craved was water. From his pocketful of Australian money, he held up a little threepence, which bought him two squashy, sticky marrow-like things. He persuaded her to bring him water, paying her first. She could have run off and disappeared, but she brought him back a jug of water, smiled shyly, tilting her head so her hair covered the side of her face. Only after completing a sale did she throw her head back to reveal herself. She had only one eye.

Peter lay trembling slightly. His mind soared and swooped like a roller coaster.

Later in the same day a special case was brought in. Two natives carried the crude stretcher. They each had such a spring in their step that the weight of the body they carried must have been almost nothing, covered with hessian, a shrunken mound indistinguishable from the stretcher itself, except that there was a great head at one end and a protruding ribcage. A man certainly, observed by the worried group of officers who accompanied the procession. After they passed, Peter sat upright. He had imagined for a moment that it was Jack – the angle of the head, the expression – the face his mind gave to that pitiful case was his brother's. Surely he was raving. Yet the image stayed and became absolute conviction. He saw – or hallucinated – that hessian mound rise up and become

Jack, who gave a sly nod and a grin and put out his hand. Peter screwed up his eyes in grief. He didn't want to go mad.

He pulled himself to his feet and started to walk, his head spinning, the wound in his chest tearing at him. He collapsed again on to his palliasse. When he next opened his eyes a sickly, greenish sunset had darkened the walls and rubble around the hospital enclosure, the shanties and piles of debris outside and the palms, languid in the windless sky. The air seemed to thicken and grow hotter without offering the relief of darkness. It was not real night, rather the earth seemed to glow and the sky to sweat. In a daze Peter remembered a compulsion – to find his brother – but now he doubted what he had seen.

The doctors continued their rounds late into the evening. Swinging a paraffin lamp, the doctor who at last reached Peter was hearty from weariness. 'Open wide! Say ah! Dear oh dear!'

'It's the chest.'

With deft scissors and hellish ripping the doctor exposed Peter's wound, a black mess in the dim light.

'Nearly got the lung, eh? Coughing any blood? I'll disinfect and bandage for the time being. Keep it clean. Rest. That's the main thing.'

Peter asked about the bloke the stretcher bearers had brought in.

'Ah yes! The talk of the town, poor chap. Fantastic story. P.O.W. got over the wire. Never seen a bloke in such bad shape. Christ knows how many more like him are still out there. He's pretty far gone. Reckons he's the last.'

'Name?'

'Jack, he says.'

Peter pulled away from the bandaging. 'Jack Tregenza.'

'What's that?'

'He's my brother.'

'The mind plays funny tricks, old son,' said the doctor,

as he would apply an emollient. 'You can't afford to get excited now. Let's have the arm. A shot'll help the pain.'

'Christ!' yelped Peter. 'What sort of needle was that? A bamboo pole!'

The doctor yawned as he turned to the next case. He hadn't slept for forty-eight hours. He did what he could. There would be no miracles.

'Thank you, sir,' Peter mumbled and turned his face to the ground. He was at the end of a row of dysentery sufferers whose purple eyes stared like terrible fruit, like plums. The sight of them warned Peter to rise and go. He pulled himself up and shambled step by step into the building. The half-hearted yellow lighting gave the place grotesque contours, charitable only in what they concealed. As he shuffled closely past, Peter was unprepared for the shapes lying on the beds there, devoid of spirit, unrecognizable as human, let alone family. Suffering made visible and manifest. And those who were not sleeping just grinned. 'Howsit going?' they greeted Peter comically. Then an orderly told him to get back to his place.

The drug was taking over and his mind rose sluggishly into speculation as he lay there shuddering throughout that night. He lamented the waste of youth, including his own. He had been buoyant, but now there was an undertow. In one almighty athlete's leap his life had passed from boyhood to old age. With his brother somewhere among those ailing men, whole generations of the family's history suddenly contracted to this one miserable place and time. All the past he and Jack had ravelled up from the knotted yarns of their father and mother, all the futures they had planned, were shrunk to the patch of earth where he lay. How different from the nobility he had expected, this strange bride of war and night, promiscuous as the jungle.

Either the drug carried him, or a current within. Thinking of Jack, memories came to him, impressions of light against the gloomy thought pattern that dominated him. And gradually a story formed.

He remembered how he and Jack as boys had gone collecting birds' eggs on the island off Gleeson's Landing. At the bottom end of the peninsula the bluff fell away to prickly reddish rocks and across a shallow stretch of water was a flat island covered with dwarf bushes in which the parrots nested. They were a species unique to that rocky promontory and the offshore island, and this was said to be the only place they laid their eggs. So Jack told Peter. Particular in the extreme, how small a pinpoint on the map that rocky island seemed to Peter now. It would have existed only in his mind, except he knew that Jack could confirm it when he found him. The parrots were sleek, unplump, greenish-brown to match perfectly the muted rock and shrub of their habitat. They laid their eggs in open grass nests on the ground, and in the laying season the tiny flat island was covered with hundreds of such nests, each with one, two or three speckled eggs exposed to the air.

One spring when they were boys old Willie took Jack and Peter round by boat to the bottom end, to the encampment at Parawurlie Bay where the crayfishermen set up. They were there for several days, and one morning the boys walked by the white track through ti-tree swamp to Gleeson's Landing, and climbed down the cliff and clambered over rocks to the water that separated the island from the land. It was shallow enough to wade across, and there were eggs. The nesting birds lifted when the two boys came up on to the flat island, and hovered, screeching, a hundred feet overhead. Jack and Peter peered at the little nests on the ground but didn't touch, and crossed to the far side of the island where they nestled on a rock, like two eggs themselves, to stare at the southern ocean. Then the birds settled again. Jack and Peter spent the whole day exploring, doing nothing, with a sense of adventure at having come so far by themselves, to such a peculiar place, and having it to themselves. They swam and dived off the rocks in water which was blue-cold and dangerous, with no bottom and an alluring swell. They found things you never found on other beaches. Then when they walked back across the island the birds rose again in the air and Jack and Peter decided they could take two eggs home, the third egg from two of the nests that had three. They wrapped them in handkerchieves and each boy put one in his pocket. Then they started to wade back.

The tide had risen and a fast current pulled between them and the shore, swift and icy. If you lost your grip on the unsettled bottom you would be carried out over rocks to the great ocean. You couldn't guess how deep it was. Jack was taller than Peter at that age and he went first. The water got steadily deeper and nudged him sideways. He kept his soles flat to the gritty sand floor. With each step the water was further up his body, until at last it was round his neck. He kept on; eventually the water was shallower again. Like trudging up a mountain, it was, but he made it. He knew, though, that smaller Peter could not make the crossing, so he yelled to his brother to wait and turned round to go back. The second time the conditions were more familiar, and made him confident, but he was tired.

'Follow me,' Jack had said to his brother. 'When it gets too deep, grab hold of my shoulders and kick us along.'

'Okay.'

That's what they did. Jack waded while Peter had his arms round Jack's shoulders and kicked like all get out. They thought they were making no progress whatever, but they reached the shore in the end. They shook themselves and grinned breathlessly, brothers, and were half dead as they tramped the long miles to their father's camp . . .

In the morning Peter felt fresher. He had slept past first light and was up at once to look for Jack. The staff were on their early rounds. Double doors which had been locked were now open to reveal a corridor leading to the hushed and sombre regions of intensive care. The pain in his chest was worse than ever. He wore no shirt, no boots. His trousers were stained and filthy, but his bruised head was friendly and appealing as he popped round all the doors there. In the last, dingiest room he found the figure whom he could not believe now was his brother. With an inexplicable sob he knelt down beside the gaunt face, and took the hand to rouse the man.

'Howdy,' he said. 'Found you at last, *Jack*. It's me – Peter.'

The grey eyelids flickered and lifted. There was fire in the eyes.

'It's me – Peter. Sh, don't talk. Cripes what a couple of dills the both of us, eh, to end up in here. Oh God – ' Peter could hardly sustain his enthusiasm – 'long time no see, brother mine.'

'Where?' whispered Jack, and winced. He had very little voice left.

'Sh. We're in hospital on some bloody island. I got myself shot down. Surface wound. Nothing to worry about. Lucky break, eh? Good thing I turned up to keep an eye on you. I bet you've got some tales to tell. They reckon you made the great escape. They reckon you'll be as right as rain, Jacko.'

But Jack's eyes were closed again and there was no sign that he could hear.

Peter laid himself across the end of Jack's bed, curled up and dozing. In time a pair of doctors came.

'He's my brother,' explained Peter.

Mildly astonished, the senior doctor ushered Peter to his feet. 'Won't be a minute.' When the doctor pulled back the sheet, Peter saw the waste of Jack's body, almost black from exposure and stick-thin. There were tropical ulcers on an arm and a leg. The flesh was rotten through to the bone and there was septicaemia in the sores. The doctor touched the limbs gingerly.

'Near-death by starvation, I'd say,' advised the senior

man. 'Malnutrition. Blood poisoning from the ulcers. He's in a pretty bad way. I shouldn't be surprised from the sweating and fever, and his orange colour, if there wasn't some damn tropical wog as well. Keep him quarantined. The limbs should come off, but it's academic really at this stage.'

'Sir,' said Peter, when the younger doctor was left with his case, 'what hope?'

The doctor laughed as at a joke. 'Are you really brothers?' His voice rose above a monotone for the first time.

'Can I stay with him?'

'He could be contagious.'

'What does he need?'

'We'll try him on the drugs we've got. Get the wounds cleaned out. Back home he'd have round the clock attention. Here the best hope is rest. Keep him drinking.'

Peter was there when Jack next woke. He bleated almost inaudibly and Peter fetched the sterilized water, poured a little into a teaspoon and, cradling Jack's head, placed the spoon between his brother's teeth and stroked his throat to force him to swallow. This procedure he repeated until Jack spluttered that he'd had enough. He slept again immediately. He must have gone far under, to a restorative place, because after a few minutes his eyes started open and were clear for a moment.

'We're winning the war, Jack,' said Peter keenly. 'Won't be long. We've only got to hang on.'

'Dinkum?' came the murmur.

'It's common knowledge,' Peter insisted. 'That's why our own lot moved up here. We're chasing the Japs back through the islands. Bloody unlucky to get stuck in here at a time like this. It's a matter of weeks. If we don't get on our legs soon, this'll be all the action I see.' Jack grimaced. His whole face seized.

'Take it easy. No more fighting for you, mate. Just get you home. But there's life in *me* yet. Whoops, sorry – '

Peter could not face the idea of going back home as he was. Inwardly he would feel disgrace if he did not accomplish his intention to become a hero. He felt sorry for himself, and wanted to be comforted. He hung his head, ashamed of his melancholy in front of Jack. With his fingers he raked his hair and tilted his hero's profile. Jack had let his eyes close. 'Jack?' he called. He didn't want his brother to abandon him.

When Jack next came round, Peter fed him more water, and mopped his brow. Jack's forehead was burning. None of the hospital staff came near, believing the case to be a waste of precious resources.

All through that day and night Peter lay beside his brother, pouring liquid into him, cooling his forehead, squeezing his hand, importuning him to live.

In the deep midnight Jack rallied suddenly and asked, 'Peter? Are you really? Where have you come from?'

'Hey Jack, I didn't tell you. You've got to get home anyway. I'm having a kid. You remember Vera Binns. Well, you know how it happens. She come with me up to town to say goodbye and next thing there's a letter saying she's having my kid and wants to marry me. A little accident, eh? It ain't even born yet. When we get back, but, there'll be something to celebrate.'

Jack smiled wanly. He felt called on to make an effort of speech. 'You're a sly dog, leaving your scent like that. Congratulations are in order.' Then Jack was gone again into unconsciousness.

Peter sat by him, watching. He didn't sleep a wink, out of superstition, as if watching could bring Jack round. In the morning he decided Jack must eat.

Outside, under the awnings of leaves, he squatted, gathering his breath as he looked for the girl peddler. His own resources had to be husbanded. Even the early morning heat made him faint. He could not have walked much further in his search, but the girl noticed him and came weaving through the crowd. Half her face was beautiful. She offered fruit and Peter shook his head. 'Milk.' His full lips uncurled in a smile. 'Biscuit.'

He waited, his haunches in the dust, dry powder between his toes, squinting at the smoky, yellow, unresponsive sky. He watched the girl return, bending and swaying, with a proud smile. She had found what he wanted – thin milk and some plain flour-and-salt biscuits wrapped, as it happened, in a propaganda leaflet – and Peter gave her his remaining florin.

He mashed some of the biscuit with milk in the spoon and cupped Jack's head in the crook of his elbow to make him take it. Jack managed three spoonfuls the first time. Once he recovered from that he lay flat as a board with his eyes closed, but said to Peter, 'Tell me about your child.'

A light passed over Peter's worn face. 'That Vera – she's hot. We were together just one night and she writes me this letter that she's having a baby.' Only a paragraph in a letter, a ruse perhaps to get him hitched. Women played tricks as did memory and imagination. But from his position now it made no difference. He kicked himself, and believed. He dreamed of mother and child as blessed creatures, on a cloud. 'She's an angel – ' His voice cracked. He coughed. Despite his ill condition, his pride made him handsome, radiant. Far away down south there would be a baby. Then a tremor passed through Peter's system and he was weak again.

'I bet it's a girl,' he said. He could picture Vera handling the baby on the changing table, giving it her breast, waking grumpily to its screaming. In Peter's thoughts, the child came into existence and grew. He saw his daughter, not as a baby but a grown girl. She was fair and strong with a wide smiling face and a straight back. She was walking in sun by a calm sea. She would be a doer, not a dreamer. She would have food and drink, clean clothes, a roof over her head and the things she needed. She would work for the things she had a right to, and they would come to her.

She would have the strong, clear mind of her generation, the gift of neither parent but of the world of peace she would be born into, where progress would be made through reason and work. He saw her laughing heartily at his faith in her as, quietly and solidly, she got on with the job of building the new world. The thought inspired awe in Peter, who had never thought much. He wished to get away from this dismal place where his and Jack's youth had lobbed, so that in tempered age he might learn from his strong daughter. Wrestle with her. But he was wandering. He took quick flatfooted steps to the bucket in the corner of Jack's room and emptied the dregs of green spew from his stomach. Then he lay down until his nausea subsided.

'Sleep, Jack.'

Perhaps Jack absorbed his brother's reverie. He slept soundly with Peter curled and shivering beside him, clenching his hands over the wound to his chest, like a baby himself.

In the morning the younger doctor came and took Jack's pulse with mildly renewed interest. Though faith in his own ability was irrelevant, he had learned an excess of indifference to the gods' behaviour.

'He's vulnerable to anything,' the doctor said when Peter stirred. 'Look after him.' And moved on.

Peter knelt by the bed and propped Jack up a little. He mashed more of the biscuit into the milk and spooned the thick gruel in between Jack's quivering lips. Jack took it like a bird, and kept taking more.

'Jack,' whispered Peter urgently, right against his brother's cheek, 'won't be long. We're winning the war. Remember.'

'Biscuit,' blinked Jack. He stuck out his tongue. Then his jaw set on the spoon.

So Peter ministered to Jack, spooning the paste into his mouth, wiping his forehead, pressing his hand with determination and love. Jack was unconscious and feverishly awake by turns. Peter lay down beside him, napping when he could. That day he carried Jack to the latrine. They passed the chaplain on his rounds, who helplessly offered help.

'Nuh!' said Peter breathlessly.

A barrel of bones stretched over with yellowed skin, bandages and baggy trousers hanging from the hips, Peter walked like King Kong as he carried Jack in his arms, who was no heavier than a bundle of sticks, or a child, and naked except for sores and a grimy bit of rag flung over his genitals.

Curly wisps of Peter's fair hair caught the light, and he gave the chaplain a rakish wink.

In the latrine two lads were smoking, sitting contentedly on adjacent bogs with everything finally worked out.

'They reckon there's cholera in the town,' said one.

'We best stay right here then,' was the reply.

There were so many infectious diseases, reasoned Peter. Who knew what another bloke had anyway?

He kept up the water and biscuit, and that night he didn't sleep for following every effort of Jack's body, as if the fight were waging in his own. He rubbed his brother's temples and cooled his head with a wet rag when the fever surged. When Jack shook and tossed, he tucked the blanket tighter round him and recounted to Jack as Jack had recounted to him in their childhood every detail of their adventure out on the boat with Dad when the storm nearly got them. Jack focussed his mind, ready to jump on any omission or falsification in the story Peter told. The story, once begun, had to be finished, and there were others, too, that carried them through the night and the following day.

'Jack,' sang Peter while his brother slept, when his breathing was troubled, 'breathe!' And Peter breathed regularly – 'now . . . now . . . now!' – until Jack's breathing steadied into harmony with his own. And Peter mouthed the words, for himself also, 'Sleep and be better.'

He prayed, promised anything so that Jack should sail through this crashing storm round his life. Peter freely admitted that he was powerless. But he also knew, or begged with fervour to change the universe, that Jack's recovery was God's will.

After the second night of constant vigil Jack was calm. With the morning heat baking the hospital, he sat up and ate the biscuit gruel himself.

'I'm okay,' he said when Peter offered to help. He repeated it emphatically: 'I'm okay.'

Laconic, amazed, the doctor duly remarked his improvement. 'I'll be.'

'Air,' said Jack. 'Could you open the window?'

It was done. In the gust of breeze Peter's skin goosepimpled.

Jack was able to talk now, and over the days of convalescence he accounted to Peter for three years of his life. His sickness had slurred his memory. Days, details, sequences were gone into a slow hazy drift, and the sharpest moment in his mind was the moment longest ago, when they had packed their bags and stood about in the dry, nipping Darwin dawn waiting for the transports to take them to the port. All their tents were empty, showing no trace of their stay, clear and ready for the next comers. January 1942. There was uncertain silence at leaving, but once up the gangplank they roared and sang and rollicked until the sky shifted weirdly in the distance and they sailed into a bitch storm. As the Timor Sea broke on them in laughing, howling gales, half were sick, half were wet, and the navy boys chuckled. When the storm passed, Jack hung his head over the deck rail, remembering his father's boat, and found a lonely companionship in the familiar liveliness of the sea. At any moment they expected the black vulture of enemy craft. Once, they jumped into positions, but all that passed was an empty junk, a floating leaf.

They came close to verdant fragments of islands at the beginning of the Malay Archipelago, and their speed slowed. As they wove among islands with clusters of thatch-and-bamboo habitation on shore, it dawned on some that their destination was Singapore harbour. When they were warned that they would see action as soon as they landed, bloodcurdling hoots and whoopees broke out.

Singapore was an unsettled place when they filed onshore that blazing morning. People were running and shoving everywhere in and out of low, grey shanty buildings, under strange trees whose roots ran down into slimy brown water, running about the urgent business of the day, life and death trading, as if no war was on. There was nothing recognizable as discipline or order, or even a laid-out city. Outside the fence of the barracks were the shrieks and jabberings, like parrots' noises, of the local bustling Chinese and Malays. Or worse the empty eyes that dared to hold yours with mournful, passive scepticism, as if they knew all, while you would never even know whose side they were on. That made the boys uncomfortable, and the girls about whom they'd been lectured made them wish they'd been there in a better season, if these were the creatures they were saving.

Their feet were still rocking from the ship's motion when the first major attack came. The boys did what they were told and manned their positions. They hardly knew where they were. Frenzy broke out among the civilian population, and evacuation started. The land attack began next night. The harbour was blitzed and the refinery hit. From the ground the enemy was unbeatable. Singapore had surrendered.

Jack and the other men stumbled sluggishly into the light of that day of surrender. They had not seen a hundred hours' action. Was this war, that it might turn and turn about like a weathervane? Prodded at gunpoint, herded, abused, they were taken into a great grassy field and left there with their drolleries while Indians worked like tars to construct a fence around them. The boys saw the thorns of wire against the sky, above their heads. They were in a city of their own now.

'Bet it's not rabbit proof,' said the bloke beside Jack, a kid from Sydney with a flat rosy face who knew all Tommy Dorsey.

'Pity we're not rabbits.'

In the gibberish of tongues they picked a recurring sound. *Jung-ee. Jung-ee.* The name of the place was Changi.

Two-storey concrete buildings, British-built and already like blackened stupas overcome by jungle and men. Spaces hacked clear for the compound and, behind, the pushed-back wall of bamboo, three storeys high and each stalk thicker than a man's thigh, frangipani, jacaranda, palm and banana and huge irregular trees that might almost have been eucalypts. Ground crawling with creeper not grass. A smell of ripe sewage that blended with a sweetness of what might have been flowers and fruit. Air that you wiped off your flesh as moisture. Every day, in a weak, buzzing fever, marched down the road to a place where you chopped and dug, without enthusiasm, without energy, in a kind of sleep, until you marched back at dark. Twenty-, twenty-one-year-olds, farmboys, too many to count or know, trudging those roads steamy from rain and sun. Friendships, adjustment, initiatives, pastimes. At bottom the most bitter cheat. Not the deaths, but the death-in-life.

When Christmas Day came, and New Year's Day 1943, and their birthdays, they knew what the date was and celebrated. They didn't really know what was going on outside. To plot sabotage was daring, but work, even if futile, even if it helped the enemy, was a better tonic. Labour kept them fit; and not physical strength but marrow within the bone kept them from cracking.

The best were sent to northern work camps. The worst were given no care and died on their feet, snapping like twigs. When the labour plans were intensified, groups of men were detached and sent away in truckloads. The Japanese were flat out to consolidate an empire. Jack was cramped into a boat with a thousand other men and shipped over the sea to a place called Sandakan. The voyage was a grim durance, and the place on arrival was crook. The men were weak and got rapidly weaker, being worked like animals there without an animal's sustenance.

At that stage Jack began a battle with himself and made each day a challenge. When he passed a day showing no signs of weakness, it was a victory. He would wake to the mauve light in the vast sky and morning birds calling, and lie with his bones through the calico bedmat against the worn ground. For a full counted minute he would stare into the universe, detaching himself so he could function as an invisible spirit in the ranks of men. He was able then to right himself and go where he was ordered, knowing that the ground was there at the far end of the day to restore him again. He survived, for a time which became one long extension, until the marches started. Of the men punitively ordered to lug rice over the mountains to the other side of the island, more fell on each trek than survived. The arithmetic was inexorable. Bashed, starved, hopeless, Jack was kept hanging in life by an obstinate, stupid fibre of the will, some link or stay he couldn't shake off, couldn't even hold in his mind. It was fraying to severance on the occasion when, for an instant, he cared so little about the guns and bayonets that he stepped off the path into the Borneo jungle, saying, 'I am the last.'

Soon he was strong enough to be helped outside for a few hours a day. He sat chatting with Peter under the awning. He was itching to be up and about, frightened of staying longer than was necessary in the wretched hospital – a staying post for death. There was colour in his face; his unshaven cheeks appeared to bristle.

'Let's get cracking,' he stirred his brother.

'Take it easy,' Peter complained, his skin showing a flaky cuprous pallor. He hated hobbling, as he and Jack supported each other, past the rows of bed-ridden men.

'Sunlight will do us good,' said Jack.

'Stinking bloody sunlight!'

Peter's blond whiskers made fuzzy his caved-in face and sepulchral smile. He looked as long and bony as some men in middle age. The chest wound had turned septic, which accounted for his jaundice and drowsiness. Sometimes he dozed off when Jack was talking. He was worn out. The doctor stood in his grubby grey coat, once white, and frowned at the young man, whose strength was spent. As Peter and Jack hobbled outside on successive days, no one could tell who was supporting whom.

One morning Peter did not come to fetch his brother. After a night of diarrhoea and shuddering sweat, the chap in charge of Peter's section called the doctor to say that he should be taken inside. There was a certain callousness among those who hoped to survive, now that the war was ending. When Jack came looking for Peter in the morning, he found him in the hospital's Rotten Row.

'Christ, what's up? Need a rest, do you?' grinned Jack.

Peter was green all over and could only hiss in response.

'You must have caught it off me,' continued Jack in good humour.

'Looks like you're the one going home.' Peter's voice was a slow rattle.

'Don't be daft, Spinner. It can't be anything serious. You've just worn yourself out.'

Peter closed his eyes to gather himself. Overnight, since Jack parted from him, he had lost weight and aged. This was his senescence. The lank fair hair, dust covered, might as well be grey. The loss of flesh made his skin sag and wrinkle. His wheezing breath came from not far below his gaping throat, shallow. There was motion in his hands and lips, nowhere else. When his eyelids opened they revealed eyes that saw only into another place, from which Jack was miles away.

'I can't take this home,' said Peter slowly.

'What?' Jack asked angrily.

'Me.'

Jack looked away and bit on a fingernail. 'Spinner,' he said, turning back with blunt conviction. 'There's nothing wrong with you that a good rest won't fix. Don't give up for God's sake. You'll be right.'

But Jack's optimism receded like a wave in helpless froth and bubble. 'Have you seen the doctor?'

'I can't even feel my chest,' said Peter whimsically in the slow crackly voice. 'I can't feel anything. Is there water?'

'I'll get someone,' said Jack.

Peter's face looked serene at the futility of Jack's concern.

A doctor came and would not enter the room. 'Don't get too close, especially in your condition.' He blocked Jack in the doorway and faced away from the bed to mouth the words. 'Most likely cholera, and that's catching. The saline drip's coming, but there's not a lot we can do with our supplies.'

'So sudden.'

'The nature of the beast, I'm afraid. You can't do for him what he did for you. One miracle's more than your fair share. Rough, eh?'

On Jack's face and in his heart was extreme distress. He saw what was true, yet believed it need not be. He had known able-bodied men lie down and die for no reason, for the horror of war, the despair in their souls when too much was asked of them. He had kept at arm's length from the puzzle. But Peter wasn't one of those men, whose fight suddenly dies, like an ember, into ashes and oblivion. Peter was an eagle -- but the lime had stuck on him, the clipping of wings, the taint.

Jack ignored the doctor's advice and went close to the bed, grasping Peter's hand. 'What you need is a drink.'

But the water dribbled out the side of his mouth and when he swallowed he almost choked.

In no great hurry the orderlies fitted him up to the drip, and he lay peacefully.

'Jack,' he murmured later, 'my cap – get it.'

He'd been using the cap as a headrest in his place under the awning. Jack brought it.

'Look – ' urged Peter, lifting his palm.

Jack felt dextrously in the traditional hiding-place behind the band, and the little thing fell out, still gold. 'Saint Christopher,' he said.

'Mum gave it to me. Yours now. Take it back.'

'Why should I take it back when you're going back too?'

'Take it. For the kid. One day. Look after her or else.'

Peter was not fighting. He was sinking down as if he had discovered something about himself and would not stay up in the world to face it, as if he had no more scope or dreams, as if his life was now spanned.

'Peter,' Jack implored, with reckless voice that cut through all circumspection. 'I don't understand. *Why? I'm* all right. We can both be. It doesn't make sense. We're winning the war. A few weeks we'll both be home. Think of that. Just think of that. You can hang on. If I've shaken it off – if I can come through the whole mad business like a ball in a lottery wheel – how much more chance do you have?'

Peter lay with his skinny long arms at his side, staring beyond Jack but speaking to him. 'I'm giving it to you. Take it. Keep it for your life, and the kid.'

'The Saint Christopher? I promise. Don't worry about that. What's more important is to get some liquid into you.'

But Peter closed his eyes and slept. Jack crouched by him. At a certain point in the dark small hours, tears began to stream from under Peter's closed eyelids. His sadness, his absence from the world he loved, the people who were that world. The life he had known, youth and beauty, and the single journey away. The life that went on in spite of his heart-broken pulling away, as a train draws from the station. To express all he experienced he could do no more than cry in his sleep. Jack looked at the glinting trickle of those tears in the dark. He didn't wake his brother. At length the tears stopped. There was no moisture left. Later his breathing stopped too. His organs had failed. The immediate cause was dehydration.

Jack held the Saint Christopher, and shook his brother's dead hand. He was numb, and hoped against hope that he had mistaken what had come with such gruesome, hungry speed. He notified the orderly. The procedures were efficient and minimal. Regulations insisted that cholera victims must be cremated at once, along with their linen and personal effects, to avoid further spread of the disease. The chaplain came and said the words. The body was consigned. At some distance from the hospital, against a windbreak of hibiscus, was the open space for the bonfires where the corpses were laid.

They took care of it at first light. The trumpets of the puce and orange hibiscus flowers were slowly opening, and their sickly odour penetrated the air. Jack could scarcely endure those flames, but he made no response. Peter who had saved his life, who had given his life, in a sheet bag such as boys might knot up for a practical joke. The wretched bundle of his possessions, all except a medallion that hung around Jack's neck. Farewell, old mate. I am the last, who does not willingly remain.

The chaplain led Jack to his little room and offered a nip of brandy. The chaplain had no other duty until the nine o'clock parade, but it was more than a matter of filling in time. Jack was taciturn, if not impolite, and the poor old chaplain was reduced to a reading. Like a faded actor, the chaplain bore with good grace the diminished usefulness war had given him, and the prospect of being entirely out of work once the war was over. But he was not a man to miss an opportunity.

' "Peace I leave with you, my peace I give unto you: not as the world gives, give I unto you. Let not your heart be troubled, neither let it be afraid." *John 14:27.* Do you believe in the resurrection of the body, Jack?'

The peddlers were already crying their wares in the balmy morning, undeterred by the smell of smoke.

'Not bloody likely,' Jack splurted. His bravado tricked him with a sob. 'Sorry.' He straightened his back. 'The most senseless fucking death of the whole bloody war – '

The forlorn chaplain spoke his lines. 'It is given for a purpose.'

'What bloody purpose?'

'That is for you to find.'

Jack sniffed the last vapours of brandy from the glass. He stood and shook the chaplain's hand with feeling. 'Look, I appreciate what you're trying to do for me, but I reckon I better go and work it out for myself.'

'Not as the world gives, I give to you,' repeated the chaplain, tilting the dregs of his glass in a blessing.

It was business as usual. Jack would not stay another minute in the hospital precincts. Although he was fit for nothing, he limped out through the gate and reported for duty. There was nothing else to do, nothing of Peter's to bother with. Except the Saint Christopher. It was as simple as that, a life. In the event there was no use for Jack anywhere, and he simply walked, round and round until he was exhausted. All day he saw his brother's face, the vivid icon it had become in those last hours of vigil. He would never forget the shining eyes that were Peter's eyes right back to boyhood, the old face that at young years had achieved its sum of wisdom. It was given to Peter, to Jack. Not as the world gives. In another way, whereby losing is a kind of giving.

Jack ended up back in hospital. His full recovery was long and slow. Gradually he accepted that he was the one with the burden of survival. He would never understand why he was the one man singled out against the odds. There was no reason or worth in him, when others finer had been sacrificed.

In time his seesawing between gratitude and guilt came to a cease. He had made his promise to Peter. That was the real thing. The commitment ran though his body like a blood transfusion, inseparable from him, changing him, bringing him to health. There was the promise which nothing would remove, any more than Peter's young death – Peter's life – would ever be removed from Jack's history or the history of all their people. Saint Christopher was the token.

A fortnight later the American commander of the town set up a p.a. system in the market place and announced that Japan had surrendered. The news meant no change at first. They did not go home at once. Not for some days, either, did they hear of the thousand suns that crowned the victory, annihilating unthinkable thousands of beings more; and more days before men grieving for their mates could acknowledge that some had lived and some had died, as if that were the final score. Ahead lay many years of civilian life to piece it all together.

Jack Tregenza lay on his mat in the salty night heat of the island's winter. Death had changed the shape of his world. To take back his brother's absence was far worse than if he had no arm or leg of his own to take back, he who was single and whole. If it came to a choice, his mother and Vera would prefer Peter's life to his. The return of neither brother would be more just. Jack decided to get off in Sydney and start a new life there. But the idea didn't last. He knew his responsibility. They might never understand in their own lives that it was not all a great cheat, a bad lottery, but perhaps in the longer view, in the life of the child, something would be rescued. Anyway he would try. As long as the world kept going.

When he thought forwards he thought of light, a calm

milky gentleness as far distant as his mind could run from the whirring purple of the tropic night. When he thought backwards he again thought of light, the sweetness and sadness of beginning for those who have seen beyond the end. The two directions of his thought, of his love, he realized, came to rest in the same place, where all his thoughts and memories merged. The place was his own beginning and ending, and also a place that would be there before and after those points of finitude, when all that his life had encompassed, and would encompass in future, resolved into one story. He would devote himself, though some would call it denial. He would never let go the line, until it was complete. He would live his life, setting it down according to his own drifting words and pattern, like a white unfurling scroll or a paper nautilus edging shorewards one year in seven, seeking completion. Eventually it would be there. He thought of currents. Then he thought of a single point, the sentinel tree. He believed the tree would still be there when he got home, solitary on the biscuit promontory across the bay. If not, he would make it so.

## 6 • SPINNER, 1941-1945

THE TIME IRENE SACKED RILEY THE hired man and Peter hung the gate, Peter was sixteen years old. When he finished the job, he wanted to swing on the taut new gate like a boy, but he had grown so big that his weight would make it drop. Instead he stood back with satisfaction and gave the cows a nod. Since Riley had been sent packing, all the important jobs would fall to Peter. Poor Riley, dismissed on account of his vile opinions. He reckoned the war was wrong. He wouldn't fight or kill. He would never have hung the gate as well as Peter either.

Jack had been gone a year then, after enlisting early in the A.I.F. Letters came from Egypt with matter-of-fact reports that made Peter's eyes pop. In his brother's absence Peter was supposed to bear the family's burdens, but Irene was soft on him. Most of the time he thought about cricket. He was the youngest player in the district eleven and secretly the best. On the sweet green Saturday afternoons of spring he would dawdle in the yard waiting for his mother to finish her cup of tea and drive him into town to pick up the transport to the game. He wore his brother's white shirt, which was too big, and his own trousers that were already too short in the leg as well as smeared red along the thigh where he shone his precious leather ball as bright as any apple. With his fingers in a subtle grip across the stitching he would mime an elaborate action, and his shoulder muscles rippled when he got it right.

When his mother dropped him outside the pub and he swaggered away from the car, he never kissed her goodbye – he was no mother's boy – but greeted his teammates who lounged under the verandah waiting for their lift to the match in Judetown.

On this particular afternoon Riley scarcely returned Peter's amiable glance. A letter had come from Jack the day before and all Wooka had heard its news. Detailed information about the fighting overseas was intermittent and unreliable. Jack's letters were one source. There were two blokes from the district in his regiment. He had written that one of them was killed in action – Riley's cousin Walter. Riley was in a cranky mood.

The men couldn't afford more than an afternoon away from their work and made motley cricketers, but they played with gusto, with no fuss. It was a good day for Wooka: Peter was the star bowler and was allowed to bowl as long as he got wickets in the bag. He took seven in quick succession. 'Whacko Spinner!' his team-mates hooted. The other ace bowler was Riley, who was understandably off his form. Alternating with Peter, he gave away the runs, and all for nothing – lame, half-hearted, easy balls straight to the bat or wide. No one held it against him, but when Wooka was batting, and the men were sitting idly on the side, he got narky.

'Bloody war,' cursed Riley. 'I'm glad I've got the sense to stay home. Why should I go and bloody die for a conspiracy of international capital? Let the bankers of Europe fight amongst themselves. Buggered if I'm getting involved.'

Coming from another man, such traitorous remarks would have been asking for trouble. But dry, sour Riley couldn't help himself. He had always been an agitator. He worked a scrappy bit of land and could never provide decently for his faint-hearted wife and four kids. He was mentally and physically agile – a lad of promise once – and it was impossible to discount the mournful beauty in his eyes. No one minded Riley, but no one bothered to help him on his slide downhill. He was barely thirty-five.

Peter was at the crease. His skin ruddy and his short curls like golden wire in the low sun. It was Peter's day and he stepped out smartly to send the ball flying like a bird through the air for six. He waved the bat above his head in exultation.

'They can't expect *men* to go and fight their war,' said Riley. 'That's the sort should be sent off to do heroics.' He gestured contemptuously at Peter, facing up again.

'Put a sock in it, Riley.'

Peter had always liked Riley. When they worked together round the farm he appreciated the man's cynical wit. Peter liked showing off to Riley, admiring him. Riley could teach Peter the way of the world, and was unfailingly engaged by the boy's charm. But naivete he despised.

After the match they went to the pub, to drink steadily as evening settled. At one stage Peter found himself leaning against Riley at the bar and said the first sympathetic thing that came into his head,

'Reckon you won't be comin' round much anymore.'

Riley threw it back with cold mockery.

'Reckon I won't be comin' round much anymore. My services won't be required.'

'Are you really against the war?'

'I don't see young sir signing up.'

Not catching on, Peter blundered. 'Jack's fighting. They're coming back from Egypt. They've been ordered to Fremantle. It's getting closer to home.'

'Thrilling, ain't it?' Riley gave the boy a snaky look and turned to drink alone. As closing time approached the men drank fast, jolly and joking, making wild, jingoistic predictions about the war, about their cricket team. Peter was toasted until he feared his bladder would burst from laughter and beer. When the opportunity came, he stumbled out the back of the pub, round the corner out of sight – and there was Riley, crouching, his head against the wall, his face hanging over his own vomit. He was sick and drunk, and more than that, convulsed in bitter spewing sobs.

Peter declared himself. 'Riley?'

'Piss off.'

The boy just stood there. Riley's head hung so low that his hair dragged in the mess.

'Are you alright?'

The man's thin face turned upwards. 'You never reached bottom, Spinner. You don't know about humiliation.' He savoured the pronunciation. 'You've got no bleeding idea, golden boy. You're the sort of person the war's for, not Walter. He was such a hopeless kid – '

Peter wondered if he should get someone. He leant forward to take hold of Riley's shoulder.

'Leave me alone!'

'Best leave him,' said the team captain standing calmly behind. He led Peter away and explained bluntly that Riley had lost his self-respect. 'He won't go to war and able-bodied mates of his are dying. Reckons he's agin the war. Some say he's bound to his family, that his wife and kids would have to go on charity without him. I reckon it's fear, plain and simple. Like a disease. For all his wit and craft he can't do anything against his own fear, and the shame's destroying him.'

The repudiation of shame made men into heroes – or became a vanity they would die for. Peter was young and vain enough to vow to avoid shame at all costs.

Another letter came from Jack, this time from Western Australia. They had made it safely back to Fremantle, where they were stocking up, waiting – but there was to be no furlough. Rumour had it that they were going north as soon as possible, not for Churchill but for Curtin. To be on native soil for a stretch, Jack wrote, was terrifically cheering.

That night, when he should have been asleep, Peter walked out into the paddocks. Still smarting from Riley's gibes, he was restless, pondering. Absentmindedly he checked the new gate which shone in the moonlight. He unlatched its chain and began to swing to and fro. He was a child, for the last time, he told himself, thinking of the names – Singapore, Malaya, the Burma line. With an agile movement of his toe he pushed the ground to make the gate swing faster. He was fit and strong. He would leave a note to tell his mum to re-employ Riley to replace him, and he would go.

He cadged and sweet-talked his way to Port Augusta by a series of lifts. Men were on the move everywhere, cocky, nervous, unprepared – ready to be helpful to others who were travelling. Peter hopped aboard the Nullabor train, but was put off at Kalgoorlie after a talking-to from the inspector. From there an aboriginal man of the church drove him all the way to Perth. Only they lost time stopping to pray.

Peter was a conversationalist, a winner of confidences, a finder of information. Grinning fit to burst on this exciting adventure, he was a young bloke for whom people would go out of their way. Jack was the aim of his quest. He expected it to be easy – and so it was. On the evening of the day he arrived on the Fremantle docks, he put his head inside a tent where three men lay in silence, smoking, booted, ankles crossed. One of them had to be his brother, black as a nigger, with hair like bristle – what Egypt had done – and the same old expression of passive curiosity and mild irritation.

'Jack, g'day. Aren't you going to get up?'

To be there was a great joke.

'Spinner!'

Jack leaped to his feet and stood with military bearing, embarrassed. His tough, lean frame shocked Peter, who slouched as though he was at home as his brother gently put an arm on his shoulder.

'I see you've come to stay,' said Jack, as Peter lugged the bag over and collapsed with all his weight on the stretcher. 'Me little brother, fellas. They call him Spinner.'

'Come express from South Australia,' the boy added, then he lay back and closed his eyes in bliss.

With nothing but a towel round his waist and Jack's shoes on his feet, Peter passed as a soldier when he went to the ablutions block for a shit, shower and shave. Spruced up then, they went out on the town. A passer-by would not have picked them as brothers. They complemented rather than matched each other, but both had the searching eyes of fishermen. Jack walked with an upright step and his seriousness made him look older than he was. He might have been the younger boy's godfather or priest, because his unexpressive presence reined Peter in. Despite physical hardening, Jack was – to Peter's disappointment – unchanged by the war. Peter loped along like a gazelle, not quite beside his brother, his rosy, golden face turning left and right, or thrown backwards, so as not to miss a trick. He felt rowdy and restless, gloriously young, invincible.

They found an eating place where the waitress was run off her feet by men crowded around the little tables.

'Some things thrive on war,' she said. 'Be going on over our heads soon.' Those were her two opinions.

'Not if we can help it,' quipped Jack.

When they were eating, Peter told the news of home. There was almost none but steady continuance. The most important account was of his cricket exploits.

'Can you run through jungle?' asked Peter. 'No short-arsed Jap's gonna outrun me!'

'They reckon the Pommies will block them off before they get down where we're going.'

'Where are you going?'

'Dunno,' Jack laughed. 'With any luck we'll end up sitting on our arses in some tropical paradise,' he complained drolly. 'Pity the locals if we do.'

Peter couldn't appreciate Jack's dryness. 'It's pretty vital, isn't it? I can't wait to get out there meself, right into the thick of it where I'll be put to good use. One thing I'm sure of – there'll be something big out there for me.'

'Is that what you want?'

'You bet. First to win the war. Second to make it an experience that meself and a couple of dozen Japs won't forget.'

Jack listened warmly to his brother's heroics. His own war had been quiet. He had seen action, and lives lost – he'd been with Riley's cousin Walter when the grenade got him, a pure fluke – and knew that war was mostly tedious and senseless; only the cause, if you could remember, gave it worth. Plus daily survival; each day planning your own affairs as sensibly as in peacetime. Jack wasn't the type to be chosen. But Peter had an instinct for prowess and, when his time came, would do something fine.

'You don't need to go out there looking,' was all Jack said.

'We're winning the war, aren't we? It won't be long now.'

'I just hope I can get through what I have to,' Jack answered flatly, 'do my bit decently. I'm not looking for more than that.'

Peter blurted, 'That's the least you can ask for. I want my chance too. I'm not going back to mum, Jack. I'm going off with you blokes from here.'

Jack smiled appreciatively. 'If everyone went off fighting, there'd be no one left at home to fight for. You'd never get away with it, anyway. They'd spot you for a kid.'

But Peter could charm his way anywhere, and he was taller and stronger than city kids who were two years older.

'You'd be wasted – ' Jack tried another tack ' – just running off with no training or nothing. You want to get into scientific stuff, navigation and that. It's in your blood.'

'What about you?'
'I'm content to be a soldier.'
'So you won't help me then.'
'You ought to stay on the farm, Spinner, for a bit longer.'
Peter gave a huge, toothy, scornful laugh. 'While you have all the thrills.'
Peter hung around while the troops prepared for departure. They had been ordered to Darwin. Jack found a place for Peter to sleep for the time being, and the boy made himself pleasant and useful. He lay odds on which group of men would see the liveliest action. No one wanted to get stuck where nothing was happening. He refused to let his mother know his whereabouts. Jack disapproved.

On the eve of embarkation there was a wild drinking parade through Fremantle. Jack and his friends took Peter along and stood him the drinks. The defiant lad, yellow curls shining and eyes shifting and alert, was the reflection of the innocent hero in all of them. 'Eh, Spinner!'

On Jack's instructions they got him so drunk that he staggered. Giggling at their antics they bundled him into a car and to the main station. He was on the train with a ticket in his pocket, slumped barely conscious against the seat. Jack stayed until the train pulled out, to see Peter didn't rouse himself and stumble on to the platform. He put up no fight. The carriage began to glide into the night, the dark, the vast desert . . . until the other side was reached.

'Safe home, Spinner,' Jack called, saluting the great machine. Somewhere out there his brother would come to his senses; by that time Jack would be staring for days on end at endless sea.

Peter wanted Jack's blood when he came to with a hammering head. The train was rattling and clicking in mockery, and everything was utterly obscure. But he could see the joke, and glumly accepted his elder brother's wisdom – for the time being . . . Anyway he had enough tales to tell; and, in due course, heady with exhaustion, padded the last hundred yards from the farm gate to the house, to face his mother.

She howled like a banshee when he appeared. Irene had scarcely left the house since he had gone, and refused to cooperate with the local investigation into his whereabouts. She knew her son was a warrior who had gone peremptorily to his destiny, his bounding animal raciness not even tempered yet into pride and guts. She was full of anguish at Peter's premature going, but gritted her teeth and did her chores. She saved her anger for his return. All her ecstasy to have him back was compressed into rage. He was scolded like a schoolboy, in a way that brought into the open for the first time her fierce, high plans for him. He would be a warrior, not cannon fodder; he would be a leader, not one of the sheep; he would train and become finely honed, not a gods' darling with bumfluff on his lip; he would be one of the knowing, as this war gave way to a new world. Peter was terrified. These things were not spelled out in so many words, but were the backbone of Irene's chastisement, in face of which his good news of Jack was little compensation. Peter said he had just wanted to see his brother, and told the tale infectiously, concealing the ignominy of his hung-over return. Irene's satisfied eyes glinted like diamonds at the son bending over his food. His weariness would wait. Though he could scarcely lift the fork to his mouth, she had farm work for him to do.

For two years Peter developed. He stood out everywhere, turning his bursting energy into a thousand and one physical exuberances, with cricket supreme, and swimming, fishing, shooting, dances – all the truant exploits of idleness and diversion while a war was fought elsewhere. There was also the rewarding routine of the farm that would be Peter's one day. No one liked to speak now of Jack's coming back. The ship had taken them to Singapore; they were scarcely down the gangway when the trap was sprung: thousands of men imprisoned overnight, the bastion of an empire nabbed. No one knew what was happening up there, as if all those people and their time in life were paralysed. They were too far away across the sea. The atrocious rumours and the worse imaginings were disbelieved. Brave young men up there, out of reach, out of sight, in an opaque, unthinkable goldfish bowl.

So Peter played cricket, perfecting his spin, and fished for salmon off the beach with a silver spinning lure. He was impeccably goodhumoured with his pampering mother, and on summer nights in 1943, with the muffled war something invisible in the darkness, he lay on a rug muffling Vera Binns's moans with his mouth, feeling her thick hot hair, her baby breasts, her stockings rolled down, her wet thighs in a frenzy, letting her drive him on till his cock's hardness hurt and his seed dribbled down inside his trouser leg. She played him, never gave herself completely. Young Peter was the god as well as her meal, and a sense of her unworthiness fortified her and held her back. Vera was seventeen then, a slim girl who went to church on Sundays to pray for the war in the straightlaced, fervid spirit that the times required.

Meanwhile Irene nagged her son about his studies and about technology. Technology was the way of the future, and Peter had a gift. The one use of war was to accelerate invention. Scientists were in the forefront of battle, as they battled with nature to make her take their side. That was to be Peter's station, too, so that after the war – Irene believed, when she thought about what was after all far away, beyond her ken (though one son had been swallowed), that the war would be shortly, swiftly over – he would reap the harvest. Irene was no fool. From watching the changes in milk, she knew something about her century. First she predicted, then she knew for a fact, that milking machines were coming. So she prophesied that human advancement would overleap itself, while her life went steadily, meagrely on. Peter was to be her representative in that process, and its beneficiary. Was she wrong, old Irene, locked within whose iron pessimism was faith in improvement through work? Nowhere in her tough fabric was there the subtlety to see that every gain brings a loss, the vision of Cassandra that not even Cassandra could live with, knowing how humanity's finest artifice turns to blood and pain, ripping up the earth, envenoming the skies, clubbing, burning or just terrifying to death millions of its inventors, as surely as the apple drops from the tree. There was no part of Irene to luxuriate in such grim anticipation. She was sternly armed in the faith that her own endurance would be rewarded by her son's feats. Perhaps she was half mad, but she kept on at him, and made him keep on, until when he enlisted early in 1944 it was to join the airforce, the princess of the services, to gain the new knowledge and become an airman.

He got his wings in Adelaide, was sighted as officer material and sent to Bairnsdale in Victoria for higher training. Good things were in store; he hoped the war would last. Then suddenly, after months, the camp was agitated. They were going north, or the war was coming down. For a last brief leave the boys were scattered; then they would regroup and the hour would be theirs. Peter travelled day and night to get to the bottom of the peninsula where they would cheer him on his way, and where there was also the passionate correspondence with Vera Binns to bring to a head.

Vera was never so courted as that weekend. He presented her with a little opal friendship ring and made protestations as he tangled his fingers in hers, his fingers in her hair. While Peter performed for his backslapping mates round the district, describing the Mitchell he had flown, she stood aloof. But at every opportunity he came to her and seized her in his arms with full-blown adoration. She made him dizzy and strong with desire, as she wriggled free from his hold and stood apart. Much as she wanted him, she would not surrender herself in a hot fumble by the roadside. That was the old country way, what her people had always done perhaps; she aimed higher. Besides she wanted Peter for herself, not with the old woman always on the lookout, let alone the rest of Wooka.

Peter still wore Jack's old cricket shirt, with soft, baggy cream trousers of his own, and white sandshoes without socks. He seemed to glow in the dark when he and Vera mooned on the front verandah of the old house, late into the night. Vera's dress glowed too, a cotton print of red carnations against white, tight at the waist, full at the skirt, and off the shoulder to show the lustrous skin of her chestbone and neck. Her face was of such perfect youthful beauty that Peter almost broke in two, not daring to touch, scarcely daring to believe his privilege that she was his. But as they stepped restlessly up and down off the verandah to the earth, and strayed into the darkness by the fence, and kissed and clutched each other, there was still a barrier to their satisfaction. They wanted to vow and surrender. They wanted a love they could take into eternity; they knew their bodies could do that for them.

But the old woman was there in the unlit house, not asleep, keeping vigil as Peter's departure approached. Soon she would call out with a croak through the bedroom window, or even appear in the doorway in her dark dressing gown, 'Time to knock off. Peter needs his sleep, Vera. Better take her home now, son.' And Peter would obey like a lamb, though willing to stop on a bushtrack as he drove her home and take her thighs and belly impatiently in his subtle hands once more. 'Ah, Spinner, no!' She would push him away, whispering to him her better plan – to consort him to town, to be with him for a last farewell before he reported back to barracks.

So it happened that Vera Binns was already aboard the bus to Adelaide when Irene brought her younger son to town in his blue airman's uniform, with her gift of a

Saint Christopher hanging round his neck. The presence of the keen-eyed girl, there on the pretext of going up for a family visit, so infuriated Irene that she showed no emotion as she hugged her beloved for the last time. If anything she scowled at the pain of grief and frustration, and got back inside her dusty vehicle to wait there for the bus to pull out. Others were about in the street. For their sake Irene took out her white handkerchief to wave. After all, Peter was going off to be a hero. He had a hero's fair and noble profile as he sat, tactfully, in a seat by himself for the departure. As the bus rolled forward, he blew his mother a golden kiss and gave the giggling smile of the child he was. For him it was adventure. The bus was still in sight of the town when he got up from his place and went to sit with the girl.

The mother wished she had not gone beyond the front gate to say goodbye. On the way home, over the rise where the sapphire ocean is suddenly visible, she was in tears, her face impassive and immobile. She brushed the nuisance tears away like flies.

In the bus Vera held her man's arm and wondered in a dream if she would ever return from this journey. Despite the grave occasion she could not disguise her delicious excitement as the bus pulled out beyond town in the pink and yellow light of seven o'clock in the morning. The grassy flats below Wooka shone with the sun. The bush rustled alive. The waters of the bay were quietly waking. She sat close to Peter and squeezed him. She wanted to cuddle him and blow kisses in his ear. He sat erect, not yielding to her, and stared as if for the first time, as if he was already far removed, at a landscape he might not see again. He shivered, involuntarily scared, and his nostrils flared. His face was set in anticipation of triumphs he couldn't quite imagine. He had been taught in camp that the way to deal with fear is not to think about it, to pretend that no dangers or inner waverings exist. They simplified things in camp: us and the enemy and the chance for a great lark which would get you medals and girls back home. Now he was off to see what it was really like. First Darwin, then probably Asia, half a world away and further than Peter's mind could reach as a bar of sunlight fell across their clasping hands and chafing thighs and he heard the low sporadic talk of the other people in the bus. He was not the only one going; and one or two of the passengers had already lost loved ones in the war. He snuggled against the rise and fall of Vera's breasts. She smiled at him with a sigh and he nudged her in the ribs. She tickled him in the armpit and he brayed so loudly that the busdriver turned. For that Peter grabbed Vera's hand and made her tickle him upwards under the knees, which he loved. Her nails scraped against his stiff uniform. She closed her eyes dreamily and sank deeply against him, filling his mouth with the perfume of her skin and hair.

The trip was long. They stopped in blazing sunlight halfway up the peninsula for tea and sandwiches in the lounge of an hotel. They stopped again at a new roadhouse sweltering in a patch of baked lilac earth on the outskirts of Port Wakefield, where an electric fan turned with fatigue and they sat at a formica-covered table to eat icecream. Vera and Peter enmeshed their fingers at the table and gawped saucily at each other while the ice-cream turned to coloured milk in the glass dishes. Tomorrow was already so close. The deadline was less than twenty-four hours away. Peter deliberately pretended there was nothing beyond. A brick wall like any other. The umpire's decision. It would have been the same if he was going back to work on the farm after the trip to town. He thought only of the wild time he and Vera must have while they were free and together. Nor did Peter think backwards, to his mother at the bus stop that morning. That she had not concealed her distaste for Vera Binns's contriving to go on the same bus to Adelaide gave Irene a gripe to get her through the day. Annoyance was a more friendly emotion than unspeakable doom. Nor did Peter give a thought to his brother Jack, wherever he was, whose prosaic letters had long since stopped. *His* war would be different. For now there was something more important before it was too late.

Saving themselves for this, Peter and Vera had both reached such a point of arousal and anticipation that they almost melted at the touch, blocking the chill feeling that lay deeper down. Besides, after so many days and years, there was the slow stupefaction of ritual about it. They walked a block from the bus station, Peter with his sausage bag, Vera with a small brown case. She took out of her purse the ring Peter had brought down to her in Wooka, the opal on a gold band. Turned round on her finger, the ring showed outwards as a wedding band. They walked two blocks to The Tintagel, a pub Peter's airforce mates had informed him of, and took their room with no questions asked. The pale plastered interior had elaborate white-painted woodwork and a grey-fringed blind with a cord and tassel that pulled down over a high window overlooking the lane. Awfully stuffy. He let the blind up and opened the window for a bit of breeze. Peter's boots creaked on the floor. He took off his shirt and vest, and his blond hair, his golden skin and Vera's rose dress gave the room its richest colours. Vera came and lay her head on his shoulder. He slung his arm round her waist and restlessly ran his fingers over her body.

'Now?' he said.

'There isn't long,' she murmured, and helped him by unfastening her eye-hooks at the back.

When they woke after sleeping, the sky was dark – a radiant violet twilight that called to them like a siren. Arm in arm, humming, petting as they walked, they roamed laughing down the wide streets. They ate a huge meal of fish and chips in Pirie Street and drank several cups of milky tea under the bright light there. They strolled the length of King William Street and followed a trio of soldiers to a dance hall where they leaned silently, indifferently, against the wall while other couples danced a frantic boogie-woogie. The music was a piper's tune leading them on, all of them knowing where. They knew when the music stopped and the lights went off and silence fell what other sounds of promises and parting they would hear, and of hope to be maintained like a habit.

Peter and Vera went back early to their hotel and continued their 'wedding night'. They had smuggled a couple of bottles of beer into their room and toasted themselves until they were tipsy. They made the most of each other, wanting pleasure selfishly and mutually, untiringly, wanting to prove by how tightly they held each other, how deeply, how intently they made love, that there was some bond of unbreakable substance between them. But at the end their hands were empty, and they said goodbye biting their lips, like children returning to innocence after a night of savage play, reticent and wondering.

So young Peter Tregenza set his cap at its proper angle and his impish face beamed.

'See you later, old chum,' he quipped.

Vera Binns blew dozens of kisses as the tram took him. She stood waving slowly after he'd gone, then waited stock-still, gathering herself with dignity, before she turned with a swift swirl of her rose-printed frock. She went to a pawnbroker and bought a real second-hand wedding ring to go beside the opal friendship ring. She put the wedding ring in her purse and took it out again. 'This is what he gave me,' she practised. 'I can wear it now.' Then she boarded the bus to Wooka, ready for the story she would tell.